Brad's Legacy:
A Son's Heart Discovered

Bradley Jesse Larson

Compiled, Edited, and Annotated by:
David and Sherry Larson

Order this book online at www.trafford.com
or email orders@trafford.com

Most Trafford titles are also available at major online book retailers.

Note for Librarians: A cataloguing record for this book is available from Library
and Archives Canada at www.collectionscanada.ca/amicus/index-e.html

Printed in Victoria, BC, Canada.

ISBN: 978-1-4269-0062-4 (sc)

*Our mission is to efficiently provide the world's finest, most comprehensive book publishing
service, enabling every author to experience success. To find out how to publish your book, your
way, and have it available worldwide, visit us online at www.trafford.com*

Trafford rev. 9/8/2009

Trafford PUBLISHING®   www.trafford.com

North America & international
toll-free: 1 888 232 4444 (USA & Canada)
phone: 250 383 6864 ♦ fax: 812 355 4082

Dedication

In Loving Memory of Bradley Jesse Larson

November 4, 1983-April 26, 2006

CONTENTS

Preface

THIS is a book about our son, and, for the most part, written by him. It is something we have been inspired to compile since his death in a tragic van/truck accident on April 26, 2006, three weeks before he was to graduate from Taylor University, Upland, Indiana. The accident also took the lives of four other precious believers: Betsy Smith, Laura VanRyn, Laurel Erb, and Monica Felver.

We had a great relationship with our son, Brad. The youngest of three, he gave us few, if any, problems—just like his brother, Jeff, and sister, Dawn. Brad loved people and people loved Brad. He was respected by his peers as a man of his word. Our house was always filled with his friends. We encouraged that by making our house open as long as the kids wanted to stay. We trusted Brad--he never gave us reason not to--and he accepted that trust as graciously as a teenager could. Brad knew that we loved him and cared about him. Did Brad get into trouble? Yes, he did, but the trouble was nothing more than the poor judgment of a mischievous student.

In a word—we thought we knew our son. And on the surface we did, just as any other parents might say they know their child. We knew we loved our son. And we did, just as any other parents might say they do. But, we did not know our Brad's heart—we had no knowledge of his private thoughts, fears, loves, hopes, desires, or his deeper spiritual makeup. That all changed with his death.

You see, we consider ourselves privileged to have come to know our son's heart in the most intimate way. Besides scores of letters and conversations with his friends that revealed a Brad unknown to us, we discovered six years of diaries he kept in spiral notebooks. We also found a prayer journal that he kept for six months during his sophomore year in college which reveals a surprisingly mature relationship with the God he worshiped. We found some unique things on his computer: a list of the people he wanted to be in his wedding and the reasons why (even though he was not really dating anyone); his ten favorite scenes from movies; copious notes and quotes he made about books he had read (and this from a child whom we could not pay to read a book in high school); as well as memorable e-mail exchanges with friends. None of his writings revealed anything a mother would be embarrassed to read. There were no secret sins you might expect of a teenager or a college student.

In the pages that follow, we have tried to piece together who this man, Bradley Jesse Larson, was. We have done this because we want him to be remembered, but also because we want him to be known more deeply by his present extended family, as well as future nieces and nephews, by friends who dearly loved him, by those who did not know him as well, and those who did not know him at all but have heard of him and the impact that he has had on people, in life and in death.

We think there is something here for parents of young people, who may feel they know their children well and those who would like to know them better. Perhaps these pages will stimulate a conversation with a child that might not take place otherwise. We think there is something in this book young people can learn—that the fears and private thoughts they have are not "abnormal;" a young person can have high standards and integrity and still be well liked, even though he or she may not "go with the flow" or do what everybody else is doing. A young person can have a deep relationship with God, one that might be envied by people many years their senior. Brad loved God and was not ashamed to write about this and talk about it with his friends. He had a mature spiritual life that was transparent in his personal writings.

We hope you will discover our son's heart after reading his book—just as we did in preparing it.

David and Sherry Larson

We have included a "Glossary", at the end of the book, for the reader who might not be familiar with some the terms that Brad uses in his entries.

Introduction

The Accident

"Your son, Bradley, has died in a tragic auto accident," said the Chaplain of the Indiana State Police—with that statement our lives changed forever in ways we could not imagine. A hush, accompanied by tears, could be heard as I relayed this message to my wife and daughter, surrounded by some close friends who had gathered in our bedroom the night of April 26, 2006.

The evening started the same as any other weeknight in the Larson household. Our twenty-four year old daughter, Dawn, had just closed on the purchase of a nearby condominium earlier that day and would soon be moving out of our home where she had lived since graduating from college. Our oldest son, Jeffrey, who had married his childhood sweetheart, Becky, was graduating from medical school in three weeks, and was to start a five-year residency in plastic surgery at the University of Wisconsin in Madison. Bradley, our twenty-two year old youngest, was also three weeks from his graduation at Taylor University, a Christian college in central Indiana. He would join his brother in Madison where he was to start law school in the fall. The boys had grown closer despite their separation from each other for four years at their respective schools, and were looking forward to living in the same town again.

Sherry and I considered our life blessed in so many ways after thirty years of marriage. We had tried to live a life of faith in God, but this phone call would test that faith in ways we could never have imagined. After a near sleepless night, we slowly started to realize that a parent's worst fear had come true for us—Brad, three other Taylor students, and a dining commons employee were among those who died when the van in which they were traveling was struck by a large truck that crossed the median of I-69 when the driver fell asleep at the wheel. The van, filled with nine passengers, was returning from Taylor University's Fort Wayne campus where they had set up for a banquet in anticipation of the inauguration of the new President of the university.

By eight o'clock the next morning, friends started arriving at our home—bringing food, flowers, condolences, and the comfort of their presence in this time of speechless grief. There were calls from many as news of the accident spread locally, regionally, and, finally, across the nation. We had called our families who began arriving that afternoon, and by that night our house was filled with scores of people, including Brad's friends from Taylor. Three couples, dear friends, who had introduced us to Christ twenty five years ago in Houston, Texas, arrived from across the country. There were calls from business associates, calls from people we only communicated with at Christmas, and calls from some we had not heard from in many years. The house was filled, day and night, with people who showed their love and care for us with prayer, support, and encouragement, founded on a firm knowledge that Brad was now at home in heaven with his Savior, Jesus Christ.

There were details of the funeral to plan. To us, this was a painful, mechanical exercise which, again, was eased by the wonderful support of dear friends in our church. These first few, post-accident days passed in a blur. We did learn from the driver of the van, who suffered relatively minor injuries, that all of the kids who died were seated in the back of the van and were joking and laughing at the time the truck struck the van. There were no screams or other evidence that the kids knew what was about to happen. This was a tender mercy—knowing they entered heaven talking and laughing! We heard story after story of how loved and respected Brad was by his classmates and peers. The father of one of Brad's friends told us he always knew that if his son was with Brad he rested easier, knowing the positive influence that Brad exerted when guys got together on a Friday night.

In subsequent weeks and months, the accident, as well as events associated with it—namely the misidentification of Whitney Cerak and

Laura Van Ryn—garnered national and international attention. God used Taylor's tragic loss to make a tremendous impact on a watching world. One of the results of this attention was a best selling book, Mistaken Identity, written by the parents of these two young women. Brad was particularly close to Laura Van Ryn who died in the accident. He is mentioned a number of times throughout the book.

After Brad's death, we learned a great deal about our son, much more than we might have learned had he not died so young. Initially, there was an outpouring of stories about Brad's character, his love for God, and his personal investment in people and relationships. In the weeks after his funeral, we received scores of letters, cards, and e-mails from his friends and teachers who knew and loved Brad. This included people from all walks of life, but primarily his peers from high school, Taylor University, the Upper Peninsula Bible Camp, where he had spent the last two summers working, and Oxford University, where he had spent the fall semester of 2005. These documented, personal testimonies about Brad and the ways in which he influenced people by his winsome attitude, humble manner and intense interest in others, touched us deeply.

Four months after the accident, we discovered that Brad had kept a diary, in nine spiral notebooks (and more recently on his laptop computer), from the time he was a junior in high school until two days before he died. These writings constitute an autobiography of sorts, written, of course, only for his eyes. For a period of six months, at age twenty, he also kept a prayer journal which reflects his commitment to try to live a life modeled after Jesus, which would also bring glory to God. Additionally, we found that in the last six months of his life he kept a regular documentation of his reflections on randomly selected Bible verses and how they might impact him on a particular day. He called these simply, "Scriptural Applications".

Though devoted to his spiritual life, Brad struggled with his relationship with the opposite sex. As any "twenty-something" Christian man might, he made a conscious effort to control the "roaming of his eyes" and his thoughts. He also lacked a certain confidence to interact with girls one-on-one; the reasons for this escaped him, as well as his friends in whom he confided. While in high school he established the "31:1 Club", based on a verse in Job: "I made a covenant with my eyes not to look lustfully at a girl." Mention of "31:1" was intended to hold him and other "club" members accountable for their thoughts in this area. The one thing that Brad wanted more than anything was a God-chosen wife who, as stated in his prayer journal, was "a woman of God whom I can grow under with You" and could "talk to for an eternity and never grow tired of hearing her voice". He had also written a letter, found in a his desk drawer, to be read to his future wife on their wedding night, although he had no idea who she might be. All of these writings—from his friends and family but mostly Brad, himself--reveal an amazingly mature young man who was introspective, self-critical, and honest about his relations with others.

On the occasion of what would have been Brad's twenty-fourth birthday, November 4, 2007, we put together a self-published paperback booklet that contained Brad's testimony, his "Scriptural Applications," and two short "sermonettes" given while on a mission trip to India as a Taylor student. We distributed the twenty-page booklet to some of Brad's peers, who had gathered that day to remember their good friend. The booklet was also shared with some of our family and friends over the next few months. Initially, we printed one hundred copies. Over the next six months, we received requests for extra copies of the booklet from many people, some of whom we did not know. At this point we have distributed over five hundred copies. We have been asked frequently if Brad's other writings could be shared. After deliberation, prayer, and discussion within our family, we offer this potpourri of his writings, which include those of our original, "homemade" version.

We know there are many books about spiritually inspiring Christians, but the best ones paint the portrait of the whole person, with diverse interests, hobbies, habits, and quirks that really allow the reader to get to know him/her. What made Brad special was that he was SO real and down to earth and engaged in such a natural way with those around him--debating about the NBA one moment and defending oil drilling in Alaska the next, all the while holding to amazingly countercultural standards in order to maintain his own purity.

This book is divided into two parts. In the first half, it is Brad's spiritual life that is most significant and is the primary purpose of our compilation. It was this aspect of his life that was most important to him; that which, we feel, he would not object to our sharing with you, the reader. We also have ample documentation of many other aspects of his life which are included in the second part of the book. They relate to a variety of events and Brad's reactions/reflections to them as noted in his diaries. For those who knew Brad, and for those who will never have a chance to meet him this side of heaven, we think you will enjoy reading about the life of a young man who was mischievous, adventuresome, studious, and winsome---all the while trying to live a life honoring to God. Sometimes that path took bends in the road that will make you laugh and even cry, all of which reveal aspects of Brad that we did not know. All were, for the most part, wholesome and healthy in such a young life and contributed to his purpose on earth—to try to follow hard after God.

David and Sherry Larson
September, 2009

A letter to my son, Brad

Dear Son,

Mom and I miss you terribly these months since you have been taken home to our Lord. There is not a room in the house that does not have some memory of you; not a day goes by that you are not in our thoughts and conversations with others: not a quiet time in prayer passes that we do not think of you, now in your heavenly home. These have been tough times for your family and friends, but we rest assured in the knowledge that God gave you to us as a gift and for that short time we will be eternally grateful. We praise Him for that.

By God's grace, you were very conscious of your purpose in this life. We know this because of the tangible things you left behind. Besides photographs of you, there are e-mails on your computer and other documents of your thoughts that reveal your wit and your academic production, as well as the mundane aspects of a near complete college career. You also documented your thoughts, fears, hopes, and day-to-day life in diaries that spanned the last six of your twenty-two years on this earth, because as you put it: *"I want to document these things because if I don't I will forget them and this is a very special time in my life that I don't want to forget."* As I read these entries, I can follow the growth and development of a young man who loved and greatly cared about others. For these private, very personal reflections I love you even more than I thought I could. They reveal your integrity and character more than could ever be realized in personal conversations were you alive.

But there is another gift you left for us, one which is invaluable because it reveals your relationship with our Lord. From January 1, 2004 through June 26, 2004, you maintained a prayer journal with daily entries. In this, you speak with God in a conversational way, as you might a good friend. You offer praise and thanks for His Word, His work in your life, and your hopes for the future—all demonstrating a faith and trust uncommon in a twenty year-old man. You pray for your friends and family and the typical concerns of a sophomore in college. You also regularly pray for your future wife, although you had no idea whom that person might be. But most of all, your prayer journal reveals someone who loves and appreciates God and His work in your young life. The simplicity, transparency, and purity of what you wrote speaks to my heart in a way I know you never intended, for I know you never thought anyone else would read this journal, much less consider sharing it with others.

That is what I want to talk to you about, Brad. I know that these were private thoughts, shared only with your God, written with no intention that others would care about them, much less read them. But, son, your insights and spiritual maturity are very special, showing a faith, trust, and love for God that is uncluttered by the worries and frets of someone my age. Your writings are special and unique to me and your mother because, as parents, we sometimes carry the self-imposed weight of social, professional, and interpersonal relationships that distract us from a more complete, wholesome, pure relationship with God and His purpose in our life. As parents who are trying to raise our children to follow after the Lord, we may never really know the result of our efforts. By sharing your journal with other parents, they might be encouraged to be more focused on their efforts in this area. By sharing this with your family and friends, they might grow and be blessed to see the heart you had for others and how you communicated with God. The journal reveals the depth of love a young person can have for God and the earnest prayers for purity, integrity, and honor that you hoped to bring to God.

Son, I feel that you have produced something that brings God glory in a way that you may never have imagined. By sharing this journal (removing those few things that might embarrass you or divulge a confidence), we want to bring God glory and honor your memory. We want to give family and friends something tangible and personal that will outlast memories and be more real than a photograph, something that may draw them closer to God and something they can read in years to come remembering you for who you were—a young man who loved and honored his Lord.

We are honored to be your parents and we love you all the more for what you have left for those of us on this side of heaven.

Love,

Dad

Brad's Testimony

SOMETHING I used to have a problem with was a thing that usually only lifts people up. It is a joyous thing, not something anyone usually struggles with. The thing I found to be my biggest problem was a feeling I encountered while listening to testimonies of others. I would hear the testimony of a convert and I would be so touched by their story. They told of their former lives of drug addiction, of the death of their spouse, of their previous thoughts of suicide, of their missionary adventures in Africa. They told amazing stories that would affect everyone who heard them. What would I ever be able to tell? I could tell of my Christian church, of my Christian family, of my Christian high school. What impact would that have? All the people I heard could tell me of their amazing conversions, how God had taken unbelievable steps to win their souls. I looked at my own story as worthless. Who could I move? I wondered. Why would anyone want to convert after listening to me? My story is as simple as they come. I've never known anything but going to church every Sunday and praying before every evening meal. I've never had to look to anyone but my mom and dad when wondering how to act. Since 5th grade, I've known nothing but Christian schooling. You could probably say that I have been rather sheltered from "real life." I became a Christian in fourth grade and my life with God grew in various ways since then - through the influences in my life, through my volunteering at my church, but most importantly through the development and growth of a personal devotional time with God during my high school years. But it was also in those high school years that my thoughts about my own testimony began. Not until my experience of moving away to college did I overcome those thoughts. My first week of college was tough for me. I didn't like the bed I would be sleeping on for the next year. I didn't like being away from my parents. I didn't like the fact that I was growing up. After about a week, God came to me. He reassured me more than anyone I knew could. He told me, "I have everything under control. Don't worry about anything. You're going to be fine." And of course, He was right. I quickly made friends, I actually enjoyed the classes I was taking, and I got so over my homesickness that I barely even wanted to come home on the holidays when I had to. Those same feelings have helped reassure me regarding my own testimony. I don't need to worry about who I could affect with my own story. God would take care of that. It didn't matter that I had never been addicted to heroin or that I had never even had an interest in going to Africa. God would use me and my story to reach whom he wanted to reach with it. He has everything under control. Never doubt that he is not only the King of the entire universe, but also the king of your heart. "'For I know the plans I have for you,' declares the LORD , 'plans to prosper you and not to harm you, plans to give you hope and a future.'"

September 1, 2004

Part 1

BRAD'S HEART

"How can a young man keep his way pure?
By living according to your word.
I seek you with all my heart;
Do not let me stray from your commands.
I have hidden your word in my heart
that I might not sin against you."
PSALM 119:9-11

As water reflects a face, so a man's heart reflects the man.
PROVERBS 27:19

Chapter 1

⌒⌒

PRAYERS OF PRAISE AND PETITION

Do not be anxious about anything, but in everything by prayer and petition,
with thanksgiving, present your requests to God. And the peace of God,
which transcends all understanding, will guard your hearts
and your minds in Christ Jesus.
PHILIPPIANS 4:6-7

I N an effort to stay true to Brad's prayer journal, only minimal corrections have been made, most of them spelling. Only those prayers of praise and personal petition from his daily entries, in the order in which he wrote them, are included. There is more to his daily written prayers than shown here, but some passages were excluded because of their personal nature. He often prayed for friends and family by name, for his future wife whom he trusted God was saving for him, and for other private circumstances of his life. For clarification purposes, there is also annotation of some entries.

Brad kept this prayer journal daily from January 1, 2004 through June 26, 2004, while a twenty year old sophomore at Taylor University. Interestingly, Brad stopped keeping his prayer journal for two reasons as he notes in this 1/4/05 entry in his diary. "The prayer journal accomplished two things: 1) It made me realize my prayers are boring and repetitive if I write them down. 2) I prayed a lot less, it seems, because I felt I had to write down everything I prayed, and then my tired hand decided the length of my conversations with the Almighty. And that's never good."

⌒⌒

"NOTHING will so enlarge the intellect, nothing so magnify the whole soul of man, as a devout, earnest, continued investigation of the great subject of the Deity." – C. H. Spurgeon.

So begins a part of my investigation, as I chronicle my efforts within the discipline of prayer. . .

January 1, 2004

Lord, I praise You for speaking to me today through the first two chapters in Luke. Never before had I realized how loaded chapter one is. Mary's song in v. 46-55 speaks of your might, your mercy, and your exaltation of the lowly, no better exemplified than in your sending the King of all mankind to the world through the poor unwed teen that is the song's author. I pray that I remember that Your "mercy is on those who fear" You. Lord, I ask forgiveness for the many sins I committed today. Forgive my attitude this morning at the basketball practice at HCS. Remind me that it's only a game.

Lord, I praise You for allowing and inviting us to cast all our worries and cares upon you. Remind me that worrying cannot add even one cubit to my stature. It is Satan putting doubt in my heart, and I pray You would protect me from his schemes. I praise You for the reminder in knowing God today that I contribute nothing to our relationship except my own sin. "For some unfathomable reason," You sought me out and allow our relationship to be. Lord, I ask for forgiveness. Lord, forgive my sins today. Forgive my laziness. Forgive any road rage outbursts I experienced today. Forgive my half-hearted effort playing basketball today. Convict me when I am in the wrong.

Lord, I praise You for the forgiveness of your people. Time and time again I say I will do something or stop doing something because it dishonors

You, yet I continue the habit. And You for some reason readily forgive me and invite me back. For that, I praise you. Remind me of Your forgiveness when it's my turn to give it to others. Lord, forgive me if I come across as condescending when I give my opinions.

LORD, I praise You for the reminder that even if "these should keep silent, the stones would immediately cry out." Your presence demands praise and even if it stopped from man, your creation would praise you. Your power and glory are unfathomable. Lord, forgive my attitude today. Yet again I struggle with remembering that my actions and attitude need to be honoring to You. Forgive my judging heart and my selfish feelings. I pray that I would always consider others before myself.

LORD, I praise You for the example You set when You were on earth. "Not My will but Yours be done." You were the perfect servant. You submitted to God's plan no matter the cost to Yourself. Remind me of Your sacrifice throughout the day. I pray that I would keep that mind-set throughout each decision I make: Not my will but Yours. Lord, forgive my inattentiveness in church today. Forgive my mind's wandering.

HELP me to not make decisions about people before I even talk to them. Forgive also the lusts of my heart. May you instill in me a lust for You.

I praise you for revealing and expounding in all the Scriptures the things concerning Yourself (Luke 24:27). It is an amazing thing the Book You gave us. It keeps my paths straight; it tells of the sacrifice of Your Son, it is a comfort in times of trouble. I thank you and praise you for it. Lord, forgive me for the sins I committed today. Forgive my vanity, especially about my hair. Forgive my prideful thoughts.

∞

FOR myself, Father, I pray that You would bless me indeed, and enlarge my territory. That Your hand would be with me, and that You would keep me from evil.

∞

CONVICT me, Father. Help me to realize my own inadequacy before You. I need to see that I am a nothing so I can realize the impact Your love has had on me. I am because of You and You alone, Father.

∞

LORD, I praise you for the blessings you bestow upon me each and every day. Wonderful friends, great schooling, a family who cares about me, people to look up to. And every day all I seem to dwell on is what I don't have. Forgive my tendencies to look past what is here toward the things that are not here. Bless my heart with contentment, in whatever state I am in. Bless me with a selfless attitude. Help me realize that my life is not my own. You are the potter and I am your clay. Mold me.

∞

BOTH going to bed late and getting out of bed late are a big temptation in college but they are no excuse for ignoring things that need to be done. Forgive my judging attitude. Forgive the impurities in my thought life.

LORD, I thank you for giving me the ability to turn to You no matter how many mistakes I make. You always call me back with open arms. Never let my pride stand in the way of such a reunion. Humble me as I approach Your throne. I thank You for such a gift. Forgive my attitude on the basketball court tonight. Remind me that I am a witness for You, whether I acknowledge it or not. Forgive me for talking behind people's backs. My heart is filled with such evil; rid me of it and fill it with Yourself. Remind me that my relationship with You is all because of You. The only thing I contributed is my own sinfulness.

LORD, I pray that I might abide in You. Let me be a branch upon Your Vine (John 15). Abide in me, also, that I might bear fruit and in so doing, glorify Your name. If I abide in You, I will keep Your commandments.

FORGIVE my being lackadaisical on the basketball court tonight. Help me to focus all of my efforts in everyday things on You.

LORD, I praise You for being everlasting. Men will rise up and fall, the earth will cease, and You will be here. You were there before the creation of the world and Your reign will never cease. It is probably impossible for me to even fathom your everlasting nature which is also amazing as You are unfathomable. Lord, forgive my tongue. I often utter a cuss word even if it's under my breath. Convict me when this occurs, because You hear it all. Forgive my mind's tendency to waver, when it should be focused.

$$\infty$$

LORD, forgive my laziness this weekend with my devotion time. Lord, I hadn't written for two days and I hadn't read for one day. There is no excuse for not doing it if I have the freedom of schedule I have now. Forgive me for talking behind people's backs. Remove that from my life. Forgive the sins in my thought life. Help me to commit that to purity not only for myself but for You and my future wife, Lord.

$$\infty$$

LORD, I praise You for the reminder that "if a plan or work is of men, it will come to nothing; but if it is of God, you cannot overthrow it." (Acts 5:38). You are the one that gives life to the plans of men, and without You it will surely come to nothing. Lord, forgive me for the sins I committed today. Forgive my selfishness. Help me realize that all I have is from You, and with giving I can be like You. Forgive my jealousy. Help me to remember that even if I don't get something I want; You have something better stored up for me.

$$\infty$$

LORD, I thank You for the example of Stephen in Acts 7. He preached Your Word without fear of what would happen to him. He received his death honorably and begged for his murderers not to be charged with the sin. Give me an appreciation for the unabashedness Stephen possessed. Help me to comprehend the sacrifice he made in his efforts to share the Word. Lord, forgive any selfish motives I have, both consciously and unconsciously. Help me to make decisions for reasons I would not be ashamed to tell people about. Forgive my attitude because it often is un-called for. Attitude is everything, they say, and only with You can I main-tain a positive and open attitude. Forgive my wandering thought life.

THANK You for assuring me that there is never an occasion for me to doubt you. Remind me of that daily. Forgive my sinful heart. When I get jeal-ous thoughts, remind me of that sin and also that if something is meant to happen it will. My heart is an evil one, Lord. Remove the lust that Satan puts into it. Guard my heart for purity, for my wife's sake.

LORD, thank You for the simplicity of redemption. Although, as Pastor Cady said, it isn't an easy thing, it is a simple one. Acts 16:31 reminds me to that: "Believe on the Lord Jesus Christ, and you will be saved." Thank You also for the impact chapter 17, verse 28 had upon my senior year: "for in Him we live and move and have our being."

LORD, bless my summer. Give me free time to read. Time to have fun. All while remembering my goal in life—to glorify my Creator.

I catch myself smiling for no apparent reason. May I remember moments like these when those other feelings come.

WITHOUT You, God, I truly am nothing. Forgive my wandering eyes, Lord. Change their focus from impurity to the holiest of holies, Your Son. Remove my pre-determined judgments of people. Help me remember that Satan rejoices with each judgment I inflict upon those I don't even know. Remind me that all are Your creation and should be appreciated for that.

LORD, forgive me for making fun of people and things. Remind me that You judge those who judge, and I am dishonoring Your name every time I do it.

LORD, I praise You because of Your promise that there is never an occasion to worry. "Sufficient for the day is its own trouble." What a privilege to have the Son of God tell you that there is no need to worry about tomorrow, next month, or next year. He has it all under control. Thank You so much for that. Forgive the tiny judgments I make, uttering words like "fool" or "idiot" constantly, as I do. Remind me that they are judgments nonetheless. Remind me that I would be a terrible witness to someone I didn't know if all they ever heard me say was "fool!" Help me to maintain an attitude that would honor Your Son.

LORD, forgive my attitude playing sports today. Remind me that although it's only a game, I should always give my best effort and maintain an attitude that would honor You.

⚬

LORD, forgive my lack of courage. Too often my mother has had to tell me to step out of my comfort zone. Give me a heart that seeks challenges and new adventures.

⚬

FORGIVE the lusts of my mind. Too often my eyes wander and there is no excuse for it. Remind me that every time it happens I am dishonoring my future wife. Forgive me when I procrastinate regarding certain things. Punish me for it if it means I will develop better habits.

⚬

LORD, I thank You for the reminder in Romans 3:10-11 that "there is none righteous...none who understands...none who seeks after God." This verse reminds me that it is not I who seek after You, Lord. I have contributed nothing to our relationship but my own sinfulness and depravity. It was You who sought me, and for that I am and will be eternally grateful. Lord, once again forgive the lusts of my heart. I pray at night for You to forgive me of this and then I go out and do it again. Forgive my wavering heart. Give it a focus on purity for You. Remind me that a lie is a lie. There are no little white lies.

⚬

LORD, forgive my statements today at lunch, talking about people negatively and unnecessarily. Remind me that I gain nothing though such talk. Forgive my prideful thoughts. May I realize my own insignificance, and may I glory only in You.

⚭

OUR father who art in heaven, hallowed by thy name. Thy kingdom come, thy will be done on earth as it is in heaven. Give us this day our daily bread. Forgive us our debts, as we forgive our debtors. Lead us not into temptation, but deliver us from the evil one. For thine is the kingdom and the power and the glory forever and ever. Amen.

⚭

FORGIVE my poor attitude when I play sports. Remind me how insignificant our play is.

⚭

FORGIVE my prideful heart. Remind me of Paul's humbling claim: that he, the most important Christian besides Christ, labeled himself the chief of all sinners. Convict me of my unrighteousness. Show me how terrible I am, that it might increase my awe at my Savior by that much more knowing that He gave Himself for me.

⚭

THANK you for the reminder in Romans 12:36 that "of Him, and through Him and to Him are all things." Lord, forgive me for the sins I have committed today. Forgive me for uttering words at dinner that were insensitive and stupid. Forgive any prideful thoughts I have. Remind me of my unworthiness of Your presence and that even despite it, You invite me in to dine with You.

⌒

FORGIVE me, Lord, for being unkind. I am a jerk. Only with You will that be remedied.

⌒

LORD, forgive my temper when it flares unnecessarily. Remind me that issues I get mad over are rarely worth it. Forgive me once again for not watching what comes out of my mouth. Remind me of the power of an unkind word.

⌒

"GIVE ear to my words, O Lord, consider my meditation. Give heed to the voice of my cry, my King and my God, for to You, I will pray." (Ps. 5:1-2) I give You thanks, Lord, for all that You have made. Lord, forgive my judging nature yet again. Help me not to fall into that trap as I so often do. Remove those thoughts from my head that my words, thoughts, and actions might honor You.

⌒

LORD, forgive my attitude when I display one that dishonors You. Forgive the callousness of my heart. Please break me even further for Your name's sake. Forgive my insensitivity. I pray that I might conquer these areas of sin in my life.

∞

LORD, forgive my prideful thoughts. I pray that You might remove my pride and fill me with humility. "None is good, no not one." Forgive me for getting in pointless arguments over nothing. May I approach them light-heartedly, if at all.

∞

LORD, once again forgive my pride. It was quite the reminder today reading for class and remembering that it was Lucifer's pride that caused his fall. Forgive also my attitude sometimes, when I just don't feel like being nice. Help me to see the selfishness I can possess sometimes.

∞

LORD, I thank You for Your Word. For the wisdom it provides, for the things it tells of You, for displaying Your character. What a blessing to be able to pick up a Book and read the words of the one, true God. Lord, forgive me for feeling sorry for myself. What selfish thoughts invade my head when that occurs. Forgive me if I come across to others in ways I wouldn't want to. May I possess an attitude like Your Son's, Lord.

∞

LORD, forgive my wandering eyes. Too often I struggle with my thought life. Please bless me with the strength to resist the temptation to take a second (or even a first) look.

∞

LORD, remind me of the truth Psalm 14 speaks, "There is none who does good. No not one." None can compare to You, Father. Your mighty works and awesome deeds are incomparable. Your glory will never cease to amaze. Countless books can be written on one aspect of Your character. You are inexhaustible, and I praise You for it. Lord, forgive me if I approach arguments with an improper mindset. May I be open to accepting new ways of thinking if I need to or a new path down a track I've treaded thousands of times. May I be ready and willing to, as Mom, would say, "Step out of my comfort zone." Only with courage that You might bless me with, may that be possible.

⚮

LORD, remind me of what Paul wrote in I Corinthians 9: "Woe is me if I do not preach the gospel." Forgive me if I neglect any opportunity You give me to preach Your Word. Give me the strength to do so. Forgive my overbearingness at work. I pray that I don't come off wrong to those I work with.

⚮

"THE heavens declare the glory of God; and the firmament shows His handiwork." How mighty must my God be that the firmament is merely His handiwork? How awesome a God could have conceived of a sky that would humble even the most puffed-up of men upon its sight. You truly are an awesome God. Lord, forgive my pride. Who am I? Who do I think I am? Remind me that I am the lowliest of the lowly. My seemingly inescapable pride is proof of that. May You provide that escape, that I might receive a humility that is only found in You. Forgive my evil thoughts. I surprise myself with evils my mind creates. Purge that from me, that it will not prevent me from growing closer to You.

REMIND me how blessed I am. Lord, forgive my attitude. Remind me that golf is a game and nothing to get worked up over. May I also be less selfish. Forgive me for not thinking of others. Forgive me for not being as dedicated with my devos. May I commit to reading and writing every night.

LORD, as I look around this airport and see people wrapped up in the business of their own lives, I pray that I may be consumed by You as much as these people are with their own schedules. May I not lose the truth that keeps You number one in my life.

FORGIVE my wandering and wavering heart. Remind me that my sole purpose is to give You glory.

LORD, I praise You for the fulfillment of Your prophecies. Your plan (or at least part of it) was revealed before it even occurred. Psalm 22 is a reminder of that. I praise You for Your reminder in I Corinthians 15, that death has no sting and Hades has no victory. Victory belongs to Your Son. Thank You for that. Lord, forgive my judgments and pre-dispositions. I have no right to say the things I do. Even if I was wronged by another, I still would have no right. Remind me of that. Forgive my tendency to make decisions with improper motives.

YOU are my shepherd. You are with me. You comfort me. You bless me. You dwell with me. Thank you for allowing us to know You and enjoy Your provisions. Remind me that it truly is an awesome privilege. Lord, forgive my tendency to look only at outward appearances. If I want to look at others as You do, I need to realize the outward appearance is meaningless. Forgive me if I bring others down. What kind of Christian am I if I perform such atrocities? Please forgive me.

LORD, I praise You for how big You are. Even if the brightest of minds gathered, they could argue about You for eternity and still not comprehend Your glory. What a God I have! Thank You so much for allowing me to know You. May that knowledge only grow more full and deep. Lord, forgive my tongue if I say things that are dirty or inappropriate. Remove even the thoughts of such things from my mind. Forgive also any tendency I might have to be pessimistic. Life is too short for that attitude.

BRAD was part of a group of Taylor students who drove to the Gulf coast for a cruise of the Caribbean during Easter vacation. The next three entries reflect that drive and the time on the ship.

Lord, I praise You for the safe travel You provided us with in our 18-hour journey down here. And thank You for making 18 hours in a van with 8 people not only tolerable but enjoyable, even. Continue to bless our trip, I pray. May I keep a rein on my wandering eyes in this atmosphere, Lord, for it surely is dangerous to a man's purity.

Lord, forgive me for the sins I have committed this week. I have not kept up with my devotions. I have had wandering eyes. My tongue has slipped too many times. My heart has judged. Forgive me, for that is some of the worst inside me. But this trip has allowed me to see some of the glory of Your creation, lord. The colors of the ocean floor. The power the ocean possesses. The beauty of an uninhabited island. Your creation truly is amazing.

"The Lord is my light and my salvation. Whom shall I fear" The Lord is the stronghold of my life. Of whom shall I be afraid?" (Ps.27.1) What a great reminder! Truly, with You on my side, I have nothing to fear. Satan has no chance. Lord, I thank You for that. I ask forgiveness once again for my wandering eyes. This cruise is not the greatest environment for a man struggling with lust. Lord, just like I did there: forgive me for making excuses. Never does that make something okay.

∞

LORD, forgive my attitude regarding certain things. Often, I look for the worst in something or someone. I look for ways out. In short, I do not trust You. Forgive me for such actions. May I honor You in all that I do.

∞

LORD, thank You for college. Not many times are we given the opportunity to witness a spectacle like tonight. A wing-wide argument over who put 200 plus worms in another's bed. This is college, and I thank You for it, Lord. Lord, forgive my laziness. You give me time and I throw it away. Forgive me for that. May I remove that nature from my life.

∞

LORD, I praise You for bringing the promise of a new day. Each morning the sun rises and the cares of yesterday don't have to mean a thing unless we make them. We make mountains out of anthills (or molehills?) for no reason. Remind me that You have everything under control. Humble me, Lord. Forgive me for my pride. Why do I think as I often do? I am nothing. I am no better than the next. Why do I try to convince myself other-

16

wise? For the foolishness of God is wiser than men and the weakness of God is stronger than men.

∞

"I have sought You, Lord, and You heard me and delivered me from all my fears...The angel of the Lord encamps all around those who fear Him and delivers them... Those who seek the Lord shall not lack any good thing" (Ps. 34). Thank You for those promises, Lord. Lord, please forgive me if I don't give all that I can in everything I do. Remind me that in all things I should honor You. Forgive me if I laugh at crude jokes or even if I tell them. I can be a fool a lot of times.

∞

LORD, I praise You for the Truth that "a man is not justified by the works of the law but by faith in Jesus Christ. (Gal. 2.16). Thank You also for, as verse 20 says, loving me and giving Yourself for me. Be the salvation of my soul, Lord Lord, forgive my pride. What a dangerous vice pride is. Grant me humility, Lord. Humble me before Your awesome throne, that I may see how contrary my actions are to Your name. Forgive me if I do not take full advantage of each and every opportunity You bless me with. Give me the spirit You want me to possess during those situations.

∞

These next four entries reflect Brad's thoughts during the Easter season.

LORD, in the words of Oswald Chambers, I thank You that "it is gloriously and majestically true that the Holy Ghost can work in us the very nature of Jesus if we will obey Him." What an amazing Truth! I praise You for that nature, Jesus. Lord, please forgive me if I sometimes lose focus dur-

17

ing this Easter season. Remind me of both the agony that came with Your Good Friday death but more importantly the incredible glory that came when You conquered death that Easter morning. Forgive me also, Lord, for my tendency to procrastinate in some things. It is a fault that needs correction.

Lord, I thank You and praise You for what You did on that Good Friday. You experienced that incredible pain and suffering so that Your people might one day reside with You in heaven. You are due any and all praise that can be offered. Remind me more often of what You endured that I might live.

Lord, "Many are Your wonderful works which You have done; and Your thoughts toward us cannot be recounted to You in order: if I would declare and speak of them, they are more than can be numbered." (Ps. 40.5) Remind me of the awesome power You possess. Lord, forgive me if I am naïve. I pray that my eyes might be opened too so that others might not look down on me as foolish if I am being naïve.

Lord, I praise You for the power of Your resurrection. You died the sacrificial death, and conquered it through Your glorious resurrection. What an amazing and powerful truth to rest my faith upon. Lord, forgive me for my judging attitude. My heart is one of the more fickle things that exist. Like the Word says, I praise You and I cut down others with the same mouth, and that is unacceptable. Forgive me for it.

LORD, thank You for the blessing of a new day. No matter how great or terrible or insignificant a day may seem, the rising Sun has never let me down. Each day brings a new opportunity. And what a blessing that is. Lord, forgive my unwillingness to be more social sometimes. Too often I have a poor attitude about getting to know new people. Remove that from me.

LORD, I pray for Your amazing grace. By it, I have been saved through faith, not of myself. It is the gift of God, not by works lest I should boast. Thank you also for the comfort You give letting me know that I am Your workmanship, created in Christ Jesus for good works. (Eph. 2: 8-10). Lord, forgive me for my pride. Teach me the humility of Paul. He, a man who is the most influential Christian in history, claimed that he was the least of all the saints (3:8). Teach me that kind of humility, that sees only glory in You and none in self.

⚬⚬

I praise You for being "one God and Father of all, who is above all, and through all, and in You all." (Eph. 4.6) Lord, please forgive me for my wandering eyes and lustful thoughts. Too often am I seeking the lusts of the flesh. Convict me when such activity overtakes me. Remove that from me, so I don't disgust myself.

⚬⚬

LORD, "whatever things are true, whatever things are noble, whatever things are just, whatever things are pure, whatever things are lovely, whatever things are of good report, if there is any virtue and if there is anything praiseworthy"—Lord, may I meditate on such things (Phil. 4:8). Lord, You are the giver of all good things and I praise You for it.

⚬⚬

LORD, I pray that I will always rejoice in You. You've given me such a powerful tool—prayer to come to You and tell You all I can. Your peace, which surpasses all understanding, guides my heart and mind through Christ Jesus. Thank You for that. Lord, forgive my judging heart. Forgive me for thinking the thoughts I do about others.

∞

LORD, by You all things were created that are in heaven and that are on earth, visible and invisible, whether thrones or dominions, or principalities or powers. All things were created through You and for You. You are before all things and in You all things consist. (Col. 1:16,17) Thank You for the friends You have blessed me with that have been invaluable in me getting this camp job. I pray that I do it well to Your glory. Forgive my tendency to be short with people if I'm not in the right mood. May I approach all situations with a positive attitude. Forgive me if I send a bad impression sometimes. May I always be conscience of the message I send.

∞

LORD, thank You for the privilege of being able to call upon You in the day of trouble. And Your promise to deliver. Remind me to give thanks to You. Whatever I do in word or deed, I should do all in the name of the Lord Jesus (Col. 3:17). Forgive me for not remembering this throughout the day. Forgive also my pride, Lord. So often I think of myself and ignore others. Forgive me for not serving men as I serve You, what You command in Col. 3.23. I praise You being all and in all (v. 11).

∞

LORD, break my spirit. Give me a broken and contrite heart. For these, O God, You will not despise (Ps. 51:17). Create in me a clean heart, O God, and renew a steadfast spirit within me. Do not cast me from Your presence and do not take Your Holy Spirit from me (v.10,11). Lord, forgive me for taking charge if it's not my place. May I go with the flow when my commanding nature wants to show itself. Control me, Lord. Forgive me for making unwise decisions. May I look to You and not waver.

LORD, I thank You and praise You for the times in my life when I am "in season," times when I am "rightly related to You," as Oswald Chambers wrote. But help me to realize that I won't ever be on a spiritual high for my life. May I learn not to make a fetish of those rare moments.

"As for me, I will call upon the Lord and He shall save me. He shall hear my voice." Thank You for Your promise in verse 22 of Psalm 55: "Cast your burden on the Lord and He shall sustain you; He shall never permit the righteous to be moved." Lord, forgive my pride. Strike me down when I stick out my chest (not literally). Remind me of my own frailty. Also, forgive me, ironically, for my lack of confidence in certain areas. Yes, it is a paradox but surely You understand.

LORD, I thank You for Your Son, the "one Mediator between God and men." I praise You for putting him through trials and tribulations and temptations, yet through it all, He committed no sin. Remind me to trust in You when I am afraid, as Psalm 56 tells me. For with You, man can do nothing to me. Lord, forgive me for not giving my best effort if I feel lazy or some other ridiculous reason. You command and deserve my best. May I always give it.

LORD, I want to pray to You tonight. Lord, You are my God and I am in awe of You. I am amazed by Your goings on everyday. You hold it all together. You organize every little thing for Your own glory. And us, me, your faulty creatures, disappoint You everyday but still You allow me to crawl back to You. And You make it all better. You give me a new day every morning. Is there anything more comforting than staring out the window, seeing the bright, blazing sun, and knowing You are a child of the most high God? If so, I have yet to know it. You bless me over and over. Even after I complain or let You down or let myself down, You continue to be there. You are the everlasting. The holy of holies. The one true God and I thank You for knowing me. I love You, Jesus.

∞

Lord, thank You for your reminder in II Timothy 1:7—"For God has not given us a spirit of fear but of power and of love and of a sound mind." Thank You also for Your well known promise of Scripture in chapter 3, verses 16 and 17. Forgive my vanity, Lord. Remind me that You look not at the outward appearance but at the heart. For myself, Lord, I pray that You might remove my judgmental thoughts.

∞

Lord, thank You for Your promise of a new day. "My soul, wait silently for God alone, For my expectation is from Him. He only is my rock and my salvation. He is my defense. I shall not be moved. In God is my salvation and my glory. The rock of my strength and my refuge is in God." (Ps. 63. 5-7) Lord, I ask forgiveness for thinking too hard about things sometimes. Often I unnecessarily dwell. I pray that the only times I dwell I will be meditating upon You. Forgive all my preconceived notions. May You reveal to me that it does no good for me to do so.

∞

LORD, remind me of the power of my own tongue. "With it, I bless my God and Father and with it I curse men." What a terrible contrast. Remind me of my words. May I be conscious of the things I say.

LORD, I praise You for listening to my prayers. You attend to me as a father to a son. What an amazing privilege to be able to converse with the God of the universe on a regular basis—tell Him my cares and concerns, vent to Him, ask Him for help, complain. You always listen to me, no matter my attitude nor my mindset or anything. I thank You for that. Lord, forgive me for not being humble. My pride is often a huge stumbling block for my spiritual advancement. Grant me the humility I need. Remind me of James 4:10: "Humble yourself in the sight of the Lord, and He will lift you up. Forgive my judgment-casting mind. What a terrible hole I dig when I do that. Remind me of the subconscious pits I dig, only to cast innocents in.

LORD, I thank You for Your Word. Your Word gives knowledge of You. It tells of the amazing work of Your Son. It tells us the stories of the earth's creation, its flood, its fall, its redemption. Thank You for it.

IN all things may God be glorified through Jesus Christ. Lord, I praise You for Your many blessings, ask forgiveness for my many faults, pray for Your hand to guide the path of this country's morality, and beg for You to impart wisdom to me.

LORD, I praise You for the institution of the church. Every Sunday, millions gather to praise the name of their Creator, the work of His Son, and the action of His Spirit. You deserve so much more than one day a week, though. Forgive Your children for not giving You what You deserve. Not that we ever could, but even our most sincere efforts fall so short. Forgive us for that. Also, forgive my desire to know things that aren't my business. Make me realize that that will never enhance my views; instead, it will detract from them. What a fool I act when I seek such knowledge.

LORD, I thank You for the simplicity You have created for us in Your offer of salvation. I am reminded of it by I John 1:9—If we confess our sins, He is faithful and just to forgive us our sins and to cleanse us from all unrighteousness. I thank You and praise You for that. Lord, please forgive me when I act like a child, as I often do. I can be such a fool. I get so caught up in me. I am so selfish in my heart of hearts and I know that it hurts You. Please forgive me when I act like that and give me the strength to conquer that stupidity.

LORD, I thank you that the end of classes for my sophomore year has come. May I remember these days for all of my life.

LORD, Our Father who art in heaven hallowed be thy name. Thy kingdom come, thy will be done. On earth as it is in heaven. Give us this day our daily bread. Forgive us of our debts. As we forgive our debtors. Lead us not into temptation but deliver us from the evil one. For thine is the kingdom and the power and the glory forever and ever. Amen.

LORD, forgive my tendency to cave into gossiping modes. May I realize that I only degrade others in the habit and I know I would be hurt if people/when people do it to me. Make me remember that.

LORD, thank You for the remainder of Your great power in Hebrews 10:31: "It is a fearful thing to fall into the hands of the living God. You are mighty and to be greatly feared. You are not *a* god, but *the* God. What an awesome privilege it is to know and serve You as that God. Thank You for it. Lord, please forgive my lack of focus throughout my daily activities. Remind me that every decision I make should be made in light of the God I have given my life to. May I take that responsibility seriously, for it surely should not be dealt with periodically.

"As for God, His way is perfect; the Word of the Lord is power. He is a shield to all who trust in Him." (2 Sam. 22:31)). What a reminder of something to strive after. Lord, I thank You for the lessons You teach me when I discipline myself enough to read, like the lessons I am currently getting in reading Soul Survivor by Philip Yancey. May I remember them and their impact.

"JESUS Christ is the same yesterday, today, and forever." (Heb. 13.8) What an amazing statement. Forever is hard to comprehend, maybe impossible for us humans. But even if we cannot comprehend it, we know that You will be the same in it. Thank You for Your consistency. Lord, forgive my tendency to pick fights or arguments unnecessarily. Very seldom do I have pure motives in those situations. Forgive me for that. May I honor Your commandment in Heb. 12:14—Pursue peace with all people and holiness. Lord, I pray that You might make me complete in every good work to Your will, as Heb. 13.21 says. Make me ready and willing to do Your will.

LORD, thank You for teaching me lessons through a variety of ways. And through that learning, I am awakening to an entirely new level of my own fallen nature and sheer stupidity/hypocrisy. I need those lessons. Lord, teach me to, when I see someone living in ways I don't understand or approve of, see them and not be disgusted but to instead see them and see someone who is thirsty for love, thirsty for You.

LORD, forgive my selfishness. I can get so caught up in something so little and so trivial and dwell on it. Help me to trust those things to You. May I realize that my misunderstanding or not understanding the situation only increases Your plan's glory. For out of something that might make no sense to me now, all will be revealed in due time. Grant me patience.

LORD, Psalm 84 says: "My soul longs, yes, even faints for the courts of the Lord." Make me longeth after You, O God. I want to long after my God and King. May I treasure You over any other. Lord, forgive me today for thinking about what others should be doing at work. Make me willing to pick out the plank from my own eyes before I aim for the speck of sawdust in my co-worker's eye. It is not my place to correct them and judge their behavior. You are the only true Judge, Jesus.

LORD, give me the right attitude and approach to the practice of fasting. May I use it as a tool for the right purpose. I pray that it teaches me humility. That it shows me that I depend not on food but on You for my strength and sustenance. May it help me in my prayer life. May I do it for the right reasons and never have selfish ambitions at heart. Use it as a tool to teach me more about You and Your faithfulness and mercy.

LORD, thank You for the beautiful weather today. I do not thank You enough when You give us a day as lovely as today. You determine when we have rain and when we have snow. It is days that bring us rainstorms that allow us to appreciate the near perfection of today's weather. Thank You for it. Lord, forgive me for speaking crudely tonight. I have found that my tongue has decreased in civility since my return from school. May my speech not be determined by my peers but by my principles. And because of You, I know what is right.

LORD, despite my transgressions and my sins and my iniquities, You will never take Your lovingkindness from me, nor will Your faithfulness fail me. Lovingkindness—I like that word. I think it describes Your attitude well. I don't know why it is one word as opposed to two but I like it. (Well done, author of Psalm 89).

My goals for the summer under "You 04": 1) Be the clay for the Potter to do His thing with. 2) Miss devo's as little as possible. 3) Grow in my prayer life. Be in unceasing prayer for my brothers and sisters in Christ. 4) Give up worrying about things out of my control. 5) May my heart for others be natural and genuine. 6) Praise God for both the goods and the bads.

6/26/04

You are the Potter. I am the clay. Mold me as You will. You are the Potter. I am the clay. Mold me as You will. You are the Potter. I am the clay. Mold me as You will. You are the Potter. I am the clay. Mold me as You will. You are the Potter. I am the clay. Mold me as You will. You are the Potter. I am the clay. Mold me as You will. You are the Potter. I am the clay. Mold me as You will. You are the Potter. I am the clay. Mold me as You will. You are the Potter. I am the clay. Mold me as You will. You are the Potter. I am the clay. Mold me as You will. You are the Potter. I am the clay. Mold me as You will. You are the Potter. I am the clay. Mold me as You will. You are the Potter. I am the clay. Mold me as You will.

Chapter 2

◌

SPIRITUAL APPLICATIONS

All Scripture is God-breathed and useful for teaching, rebuking, correcting,
and training in righteousness, so that the man of God may be
thoroughly equipped for every good deed
2 TIMOTHY 3:16, 17

We found this file on Brad's computer about a year after his death. He kept it most days of the last five months of his life. It would appear that he randomly selected a verse from Scripture and then reflected how that verse might impact him that day. It has been said that each day of our lives we make choices about how we are going to live that day. It would seem that Brad wanted to make choices that would please God. Of particular interest are his thoughts on the sovereignty of God as reflected in his last entry, two days before he died.

11.25.2005

Verse: II Corinthians 2.15: "For we are to God the fragrance of Christ among those who are being saved and among those are who perishing."

Application: What do I smell like? How often do I think about the fact that my actions are helping every person I encounter to their eternal destination? Everything I do can have eternal consequences – not just for me but for others, too. I know that often I smell like stinking filth. The goal: smell like fresh, Florida citrus and brighten the lives of others.

11.27.05

Verse: II Corinthians 4.5: "For we do not preach ourselves, but Christ Jesus the Lord..."

29

Application: I should determine to never push my own personal beliefs about the truth on someone. What I mean by that is this: never is it necessary for me to lambaste someone who holds a different predestination belief, or a different belief about Christ's return. The message is Christ, and when I try to pump my personal jazz in there, I am not giving that message. I am giving myself.

11.28.05

Verse: II Corinthians 5.4: "For we who are in this tent groan, being burdened, not because we want to be unclothed, but further clothed, that mortality may be swallowed up by life."

Application: What a baller verse. First of all, ever since I heard it at camp, I love thinking of the human body as a "tent." It really gets the message across about the temporality of this life. I also love this verse because of the thought of being "further clothed" one day. I need to live like that. As though one day, I will be further clothed than I am now. Right now, my tent is but a burden. Then, my further clothes will be swallowing up my other trash.

11.29.05

Verse: II Corinthians 5.20: "Now then, we are ambassadors for Christ, as though God were pleading through us..."

Application: How often do I recognize that I am the mouthpiece of God, or rather one of many, I guess. Not very often. I want to keep this in mind throughout my day, recognizing that I am an ambassador for the Almighty. What a privilege. What an honor. What a responsibility!

11.30.05

Verse: II Corinthians 6.11: "O Corinthians! We have spoken openly to you, our heart is wide open."

Application: Open your heart up, you Scrooge! Too often I have my heart closed to a person before I have even exchanged a word with them. I am a cruel, cruel man and don't give people a chance. Also, open your heart up to ideas. You are a close-minded fool in many of your ways. Change that or be doomed to the same faulty ideas you hold today, in your prideful youth.

12.01.05

Verse: Psalm 46.10: "Be still, and know that I am God."

Application: I love this verse. Perhaps I love it because it is something I aspire to do often and fail miserably at doing so. I want to be still before Him. I want to quiet my heart before Him. I want to sit in His presence, be in awe at Him, recognizing that He is God.

12.03.05

Verse: II Corinthians 8.3,5: "For I bear witness that according to their ability, yes, and beyond their ability, they were freely willing [to give]... but they gave themselves to the Lord and then to us by the will of God."

Application: I don't know if I have ever given beyond my ability. That is a discomforting thought. I'm not just talking financially, because I don't want to limit this passage to talking about financial means only. I want to give of myself more. And when I do it, I want to do it like the churches of Macedonia that Paul speaks of here. First giving myself to the Lord, and then to others by His will. That should be a goal.

12.04.05

Verse: II Corinthians 9.7: "So let each one give as he purposes in his heart, not grudgingly or of necessity; for God loves a cheerful giver."

Application: God does not want what I have to offer if I only grudgingly or obligatorily offer it; what good is an unchanged heart? That is what he wants after all. God's concern is HOW we give, not how much.

12.05.05

Verse: Psalm 49.16-17: "Do not be afraid when one becomes rich, When the glory of his house is increased; For when he dies he shall carry nothing away; His glory shall not descend after him."

Application: I like this image, although it doesn't seem to bode well for rich people like me. Riches, power, glories of this world mean jack. Those who have them can't "descend" with them, giving a little hint about where that person is headed. May I find my riches and glories not in this world.

12.06.05

Verses: Numbers 11

Application: This passage I found just plain confusing. Verses 1-10 is basically about the people complaining about how they are sick of manna and want some meat. Then Moses goes to the Lord and asks for death because he cannot bear the burden of their complaining alone (as though he had even been doing that!). So the Lord's anger then shows itself in this kind of attitude: "You want meat, you say? I'll give you meat. You'll have meat coming out your ears (actually, nostrils according to verse 20). Moses, being Moses, has to go ahead and doubt that the Lord can even do it. "Where's the meat gonna come from?" Of course. But then the Lord sends the meat he promised in the form of quail. The people who had asked for it angered the Lord, though, so he killed them. Does that seem strange to anyone else? I liked the passage, though. Not much application, but still a worthwhile commentary, I thought.

12.07.05

Verse: II Corinthians 12.15: "And I will very gladly spend and be spent for your souls..."

Application: This continues the thing Paul has been discussing through-out this book, I think. That idea that we are to suffer with sufferers, be joyful with the joyous, etc. I really like that idea. If we are one body, then we should act that way. We should be spending ourselves for the other members.

12.27.05

Verse: Psalm 63.6: "When I remember You on my bed, I meditate on You in the night watches."

Application: Rarely do I meditate on God. One of the many spiritual disciplines on which I still have a lot of work to do. This verse I guess serves as a reminder that any spare moment (or moments that are set aside for the specific activity) would be valuably spent if I used them for dwelling upon the Almighty.

12.28.05

Verse: Galatians 2.6: "… God shows personal favoritism to no man…"

Application: I love this piece because it reminds me of the story in What's So Amazing About Grace? that I read to the fam on Christmas Eve. The summary of God's love is short and poignant: "We're all bastards, but God loves us anyway." Like the story communicates, unless God loves the murderers just as much as he loves the do-gooders, then the Gospel means nothing. God shows no favoritism. We're all bastards, but God loves us anyway.

12.29.05

Verse: Numbers 32.23: "… be sure your sin will find you out."

Application: Anything I try to keep just between me and I will come out. And usually it will be revealed in a painful fashion. There are two ways to avoid such an outcome. One is to not sin at all. This would be great, but not exactly the most likely. Option 2 is to be open and honest about mistakes I make. This promises to be humbling but far more rewarding than keeping something caged in. Trust it.

01.04.06

Verse: Psalm 68.19: "Blessed be the Lord, who daily loads us with benefits, the God of our salvation!"

Application: What a baller verse. He really does load us up. I am digging that phrase quite a bit. He has basically satisfied every potential need I have ten times over and then some. He "LOADS" us. I remember listening to a Stuart sermon in Oxford, and he was saying how people who are asked to recount their blessings (or "benefits") usually list material possessions. But His benefits are so much more than that. He's given me a solid mind, good work ethic, health, relationships, etc. Man, wow.

01.05.06

Verse: Deuteronomy 1.31: "and in the wilderness, where you saw how the Lord your God carried you, as a man carries his son…"

Application: How huge is this verse. What a baller allusion. As a man carries his son, so the Lord carries his people. That is quite encouraging. And this promise comes in a description of one of the most difficult times for God's people – their wandering in the wilderness. Imagine how insignificant my troubles are in comparison to that.

01.06.06

Verse: Deuteronomy 2.7: "These forty years the Lord your God has been with you; you have lacked nothing."

Application: The Lord will provide. That is basically what this whole verse is about, I think. Even though the Israelites had been disobedient and the Lord had punished them with forty years in the wilderness, he never left them. In fact, he gave them everything they needed so that they "lacked nothing" the entire time. That is pretty sweet, I think.

01.07.06

Verse: "Bear one another's burdens, and so fulfill the law of Christ."

Application: I read this chapter for the second day in a row and somehow, I missed this verse the first time, despite the familiarity of the phrase and concept. This is so important, though, and I often forget it. The body of Christ is not one, but is many, and we are called to bear one another's burdens together. This requires sharing with others things that are affecting me and inviting them to share themselves with me.

01.09.06

Verse: Deuteronomy 4.4: "But you who held fast to the Lord your God are alive today, every one of you."

Application: This is in the portion of Scripture when Moses is commanding the obedience of the Israelites either following or during their time in the wilderness. That part doesn't relate to me as much, but I took it for something else. If I can "hold fast" to the Lord, he will certainly hold fast to me. The Lord is faithful. Even when I do screw up and take another path, He will always take me back whenever I will allow him to. That is the power of the love of God.

01.10.06

Verse: Deuteronomy 4.24: "For the Lord your God is a consuming fire, a jealous God."

Application: I sometimes forget this attribute of God. God hates it so much when I give myself to something other than him. He becomes like a consuming fire. Like the bonfire on Guy Fawkes Day at Oxford. Huge and unquenchable, ready to consume all in its path. Why would I ever want to stir up those feelings in God? It would only be fool-hardy to ever give myself to something other than him.

01.15.06

Verse: Deuteronomy 7.6: "For you are a holy people to the Lord your God; the Lord your God has chosen you to be a people for Himself, a special treasure above all the peoples on the face of the earth."

Application: I love God. I love God and what he does to me. For some reason today, in my preparatory prayer, I was filled with a desire to proclaim my love of God. So I did, and I repeated "I love you" several times to myself. Then I go and read this verse. He has chosen me, as verse 7 goes on to say, "because the Lord loves you." Baller. What more could I have going for me.

01.16.06

Verse: Deuteronomy 8.4: "Your garments did not wear out on you, nor did your foot swell these forty years."

Application: Here, the Israelites are hearing about their last forty years. How often do we barely notice the many blessings of God. He sent them to the wilderness "that He might humble you and that he might test you, to do you good in the end," and much of what he received in return was complaining. They probably never acknowledged the little blessings – like having adequate clothing and never having sore feet. I know I do this often, and I want to know about the things I take for granted, because God has been so faithful in providing them. May I work on that.

01.17.06

Verse: Deuteronomy 9.21: "Then I took your sin, the calf which you had made, and burned it with fire and crushed it and ground it very small, until it was as fine as dust; and I threw its dust into the brook that descended from the mountain.

"Application: Here, I think Moses answers the question about what to do when I have sin in my life. I need to absolutely destroy it. Obliterate it. Decimate it. Grind it into a fine powder and then throw it down the river. That way, I will never again consider allowing it to take me over again. Sin is too powerful, too dangerous, to let that happen.

01.18.06

Verses: Micah 6.8: "He has shown thee, O man, what is good and what the Lord requires of thee, but to do justly and to love mercy and to walk humbly with thy God."

Application: The genius amongst men, Dr. Winfried Corduan, spoke this morning on this verse in chapel. So often, we as believers, get so caught up in the gimmicks and superstitions of Christianity – the "how to's" put out by the newest Christian book. Or sometimes we get focused on non-believers and their dedication to their beliefs. We are doing just fine. If we want to follow the Lord, we have three simply steps. Do justly. Love mercy. And walk *humbly* with Him. As Pastor Cady used to say, it's simple but not easy.

01.23.06

Verse: Psalm 79.13: "So we, Your people and sheep of Your pasture, will give You thanks forever; We will show forth Your praise to all generations."

Application: I just liked this verse today because it is a good reminder for me right now for some reason. I am one of the sheep of God's pasture. He cares for me and seeks me when I'm lost and loves me even when I do try to run away. There is no better position to be in than in the loving arms of the Great Shepherd.

01.31.06

Verse: Philippians 2.3: "Do nothing out of selfish ambition or vain conceit, but in humility consider others better than yourselves."

Application: This verse has always been important to me, or at least for the last year or two. It is so important and yet so difficult. I have had it memorized for a good bit now, but still, it is so easy to ignore the principle behind it. That is the one thing about memorization. As great as it is for me, it sometimes depreciates the personal value of the verse, since it is thought of so many times that it is often forgotten what the real meaning is behind it.

02.01.06

Verse: Deuteronomy 16.12: "And you shall remember that you were a slave in Egypt, and you shall be careful to observe these statutes."

Application: This is just a reminder to always remember what the Lord has brought me through. Remember the past; do not forget it, for it has been a gift from above. And I should be thankful for it, good or bad.

02.02.06

Philippians 1.12: "Now I want you to know, brothers, that what has happened to me has really served to advance the gospel. As a result, it has become clear throughout the whole palace guard and to everyone else that I am in chains for Christ."

Application: How much of a baller must Paul have been for the "whole palace guard" to recognize who he was in chains for. Of course, normally the palace guard probably didn't even notice a blasted thing about the prisoners, except that they probably smelled a little bit like feces or that they desperately needed some dental care (I'm assuming). But Paul certainly grabbed their attention. And he didn't let go until they knew why he was there and whom he was suffering for.

02.03.06

Verse: Deuteronomy 18.15: "The Lord your God will raise up for you a Prophet like me from your midst, from your brethren. Him you shall hear."

Application: I just kind of like this verse that foretells Christ's coming. I don't think I've ever really heard it before or noticed it. This is the verse that Stephen uses in Acts 7 in support of his claim that Jesus is God's Son. What a title, man. God's Son. That is some smooth action.

02.04.06

Verse: Philippians 2.12-13: "... continue to work out your salvation with fear and trembling, for it is God who works in you to will and to act according to his good purpose."

Application: I have been thinking about this recently, due to Corduan in class talking about how mistitled his book is: No Doubt About It. As he said, "If there were no doubt about it, then there would be no need for a book." The Lord wants me to work out my faith, question it, doubt it if I have to; it's something we all go through, and the real tragedy is thinking there is something wrong with me or with the act of doubting itself.

02.05.06

Verse: Psalms 85.9: "Surely His salvation is near to those who fear Him."

Application: This is something that was talked about a bit in something I recently read: the fear of the Lord. It's not something I am entirely sure I understand, but I can acknowledge that I need to try harder to attain it. It is because of the promises of verses like this that it is essential for me to do so.

02.06.06

Verse: John 3.3: "Jesus answered and said to [Nicodemus], 'Most assuredly, I say to you, unless one is born again, he cannot enter the kingdom of God.'"

Application: Sometimes, I am so harsh with the cliché Christian terms. Although I don't specifically remember this, I am sure that I have condescendingly viewed the term "born again," not realizing that it is completely Biblical, from the mouth of Christ, even. And it is a really great term. It describes the process perfectly. One needs to be born again in order to enter.

02.08.06

Verse: I Corinthians 13.3: "And though I bestow all my goods to feed the poor, and though I give my body to be burned, but have not love, it profits me nothing."

Application: This is straight truth about how God feels about works. You can do all the "good" things possible and follow every rule in the book, but if you aren't doing it with the right heart, one of love, then you aren't doing a thing at all. I think this is one of the strongest things Christianity has going for itself. It doesn't want your money. It doesn't want your works. It wants your brokenness. It wants your heart. It wants you to be filled with the love of Christ so that it can be shared amongst all men.

02.10.06

I just had one of the most amazing prayer experiences of my life. It started right after I sent an email to the boys of the UPrising. Here's what I wrote:

Hello again, good sirs.

I have some words to share with you. Upon reading Gordon's email last week, I was inspired to write a little something of my own. Like G, it is often hard for me to open up about certain aspects of myself. I agree with him that I am a rather private person, and that has helped me in many situations, but it has often hindered the potential of my relationships with people. So I thought I would bounce something off you boys regarding something I have been thinking about lately. Sadly, I have to say that my "one on one" time with God has been struggling as of late. I pray less than I used to and I take a less serious approach to reading Scripture regularly. (This is not to say that I never do these things, because I still certainly do.) Here is the problem, though: I am loving life right now more than I have in awhile. I go to bed each night wondering if it would be possible for my life to be more enjoyable than it is right now. I remember often wondering over the past year or two, "What would change in my life if I never read the Bible? How does the Word affect me everyday?" It was almost a game that I wanted to play, to not read the Bible for a month or something just to see if everything would go to crap. I know that sounds terrible, but I have to be real about what I have thought. I've never done it, however, but in my desire to find the answer to the question "How does the Word/prayer change me?", I began to record a journal of sorts about a verse I had read in the Word that day and how it could apply to my life. It has been valuable but certainly not life-changing. My question to you guys is this: how does the Word or prayer or worship or what have you change you on a day to day basis? I am not sure of the answer for myself. But I certainly want to hear what you have to say, if anything. Of course, like all of you, I need prayer. And I will be praying for you. God bless the UPrising. (That's pretty tight, how I did that, huh? ...with the "you pee" in caps. You like that, don't you...)

Fondly yours,
Bradley J. Larson

I was real with them and then I was real with God. Of course, He knew it all along, but maybe I didn't. I wasn't aware that these were some of my thoughts until I put finger to keyboard. Then it came out. And I am pretty happy about it all. I am not someone who often (if ever) experiences the supernatural aspect of faith in a dramatic fashion. I am so logical and rational that maybe my mind is not geared toward that kind of thing. But that prayer experience was awesome for me. It's true, there was no overpowering or all-encompassing feeling that overtook me while I was praying. But I was real and I was intimate with the Almighty, and it felt damn good. Thank You, Jesus. I love You.

02.11.06
There were a bunch of great verses in today's reading, so I think I'll just share those.

Deuteronomy 23.5: "... but the Lord your God turned the curse into a blessing for you, because the Lord your God loves you."

Psalm 90.4: "For a thousand years in Your sight are like yesterday when it is past."

Psalm 90.8: "You have set our iniquities before You, our secret sins in the light of Your countenance."

Psalm 90.12: "So teach us to number our days, that we may gain a heart of wisdom."

02.12.06

Verse: Psalm 90.12: "So teach us to number our days, that we may gain a heart of wisdom."

Application: I decided to speak my mind regarding this verse that I first went over yesterday. Teach us to number our days, it says, that we might gain a heart of wisdom. We are not going to live forever, and nothing I can do or I think I can do will ever change that. My end is coming just as soon as the next guy's, and the real wisdom can be found in recognizing that. So may I always remember that I am feeble. I am weak. I am infirm. May I never attempt to trick myself into disbelieving that.

02.13.06

There is nothing I can do to make God love me less. Nothing. That was the theme from tonight's Nooma video. This is the same lesson from Yancey's WSAAG (*What's So Amazing About Grace?*) There is nothing I can possibly do or say or think or feel or act upon or inflict on someone or anything to make God love me any less. I don't get that a lot of times. I am all embarrassed or scared or ashamed to go to God after I disobey Him. Especially after I wittingly disobey Him, which has happened. That is so despicable. That is cheap grace, or at least that is a fitting term to describe my attitude about the whole thing. I treat it cheaply, as though it is a tool that I am free to take advantage of. I disgust me.

02.14.06

Verse: Acts 1.23-24: "And they proposed two: Joseph called Barsabbas, who was surnamed Justus, and Matthias. And they prayed and said, "You, O Lord, who know the hearts of all, show which of these two You have chosen."

Application: What a great model for decision making. The ~~disciples~~ apostles needed to choose another member, once Judas off-ed himself, and they had 2 choices: Matthias and Joseph called Barsabbas. They pray and ask for guidance. (Then they cast lots.) And they have their man. The power of prayer is a mysterious and wonderful thing.

02.15.06

Verse: Acts 2.44-45: "Now all who believed were together, and had all things in common, and sold their possessions and goods, and divided them among all, as anyone had need."

Application: This is how the church should act. It is not a church that quibbles over worship styles and/or the junior high pastor. It is not one filled with hypocrites and legalists. It is one who believes together. It does not have to be a church that agrees on Calvinist principles or one whose creation doctrine can be defended by each and every member of the church. But it is still one that is together, ready and willing to sacrifice for the next person. What a challenge.

02.16.06

I just finished reading the Prodigal Son re-told excerpt from the "Lovesick Father" chapter in Yancey's What's So Amazing About Grace?. And I wept like a child. I've read that piece at least five times, tearing up in every one except when I read it to the fam this past Christmas Eve. I was barely able to hold back then. This time, I didn't hold back. It's like I discovered this summer at camp when I shared with the family campers. Our God is crazy. What is he thinking? He is absolutely crazy about us. Us- the beat up, the broke down, the bedraggled. And He loves us in an out-of-control fashion. Maybe I am repeating what I said this summer, but I don't really care. This is too crucial to my understanding of God and who He is and what He feels towards me. I serve a Looney. A Looney who is looney over me.

02.17.06

Acts 3.12: "When Peter saw this, he said to them: 'Men of Israel, why does this surprise you? Why do you stare at us as if by our own power or godliness we had made this man walk?'"

Application: Peter made no bones about the fact that he had little, if anything, to do with this miracle (of healing the crippled beggar). And he calls the amazed crowd on the whole thing. They are clueless on the whole operation if they are silly enough to imagine that it was Peter who actually did the miracle, and not the Christ that lives inside him. It was not by their own power, nor their own godliness. It was their God, through their bodies.

02.19.06

Acts 4.31: "And when they had prayed, the place where they were assembled together was shaken; and they were all filled with the Holy Spirit, and they spoke the word of God with boldness."

Application: Amazing verse. Amazing chapter. Amazing book. I noted like three things in this chapter that were baller statements about the early church. I thought of the Uprising upon reading this specific one. Can we shake the place U.P.? We can if we are filled with the Holy Spirit, and He is willing to do a work through us. And we are willing to speak truth in boldness. I like this verse.

02.20.06

Acts 5.4: "... Why have you conceived this thing in your heart? You have not lied to men but to God."

Application: These are the words that Peter spoke to the lying Ananias before he "fell down and breathed his last." That is just a really powerful thought to me. In dealing with something like dishonesty before the Lord, I must understand that I am basically lying to His face. It does me no good to not be completely honest with Him. Understand that I am not lying to men but to God.

02.21.06

Psalm 96.9: "Oh, worship the Lord in the beauty of holiness! Tremble before Him, all the earth."

How often do I do tremble before the Lord? I can tell you that I cannot recall ever doing it. There is something wrong with that, I imagine. What can I do to make me tremble before Him? Perhaps meditation on who God is and what He has done for me would be good. You know, maybe last week, when I was driven to tears by the retelling of the "Parable of the Prodigal Son", maybe that was an instance of trembling before the Lord. Perhaps I do do it, but just not enough. Obviously, I can always do more. Never get stagnant.

02.22.06

Acts 7. What an amazing chapter. Stephen is here before this council of religious leaders, and he's asked whether or not he has said these things about Jesus. Chapter 6 says that all who sat in the council looked "steadfastly at him, [and] saw his face as the face of an angel." Baller. Then he goes on this insane diatribe about the history of the Lord's people, from Abraham down to Christ himself. If nothing else, this demonstrated an incredible knowledge of Scripture and history. Then you read the peoples' reactions. Verse 54 says, "... they were cut to the heart." So what do they do? Stone him, of course. Makes perfect sense, doesn't it? Get rid of this angel-looking dude that just blew us away with his speech. He can't be good for anything.

02.23.06

Deuteronomy 33.50: (to Moses) "... and die on the mountain... because you trespassed against Me among the children of Israel at the waters of Meribah Kadesh, in the Wilderness of Zin, because you did not hallow Me in the midst of the children of Israel. Yet you shall see the land before you, though you shall not go there, into the land which I am giving to the children of Israel."

The Lord is not messing around. If you don't hallow Him, things will not turn out well for you. Moses's whole second life was built around the promise of entering the promised land, a land flowing with milk and honey. He messes up and his chance to enter it is gone. He can see it, but he will not be entering it. He will die on the mountainside (which by the way is a weird thing to tell a man before he goes up a hill).

02.24.06

Acts 8.34-35: "The eunuch asked Philip, 'Tell me, please, who is the prophet talking about, himself or someone else?' Then Philip began with that very passage of Scripture and told him the good news about Jesus."

Awesome, awesome, awesome. This chapter is baller. I love several of the verses, but this one especially stuck out to me. I think too often that people have the attitude or style of preaching at people. The NKJV says that Philip "preached Jesus to him." I like that much better. First, you are preaching TO the person instead of AT him. And more importantly, you are preaching JESUS. JESUS JESUS JESUS. That name is awesome. Jesus.

02.26.06

Deuteronomy 34.10-12: "Since that time no prophet has risen in Israel like Moses, whom the LORD knew face to face, for all the signs and wonders which the LORD sent him to perform in the land of Egypt against Pharaoh, all his servants, and all his land, and for all the mighty power and for all the great terror which Moses performed in the sight of all Israel."

Tight string of verses honoring the man, the myth, the legend... Moses. No prophet has arisen since this cat. The Lord knew him face to face (perhaps the most amazing compliment in the Bible, if it can be considered that). Signs, wonders, mighty power, great terror. What it all adds up to is quite the resume. Just an impressive dude that is perhaps my favorite Bible character. I do really like Joseph though. But I can't tell if that's just Andrew Lloyd Webber influence.

03.01.06

Acts 11.17: "... who was I that I could withstand God?"

I just realized that this verse which I memorized this summer was taken pretty much out of context (I guess as all memory verses are), but I still like the message, even (or especially) in context. Peter is talking about how the Spirit fell upon a group after he was speaking to them. He observed that if God gave them the same gift that he and the other disciples had received, who was he to stand in the way of that? I think that is something that Christians get caught up in a bit these days. We don't just want people to change; we want them to change to what we want them to be. That is pretty much awful. God will do the deed, and who are we to get in the way of what He is doing?

03.02.06

Acts 12.23: "Then immediately an angel of the Lord struck [Herod Agrippa], because he did not give glory to God. And he was eaten by worms and died."

Intense verse. God does not take pride lightly. He is praised as a god and not as a man in the preceding verse, and apparently, he does nothing to stop such praise. So an angel strikes him, and he dies an embarrassing and painful death. According to my Bible, being eaten by worms was considered to be one of the most disgraceful ways to die. Remember that God is active and powerful and potent. He does not mess around.

04.20.06

Verse: Romans 6.11: "In the same way, count yourselves dead to sin but alive to God in Christ Jesus."

Application: A lot of times, I think I misunderstand Christ's work on the cross. He did what He did not so that I can sin more or not worry about going to hell when I do sin. He did it so that sin would no longer be an issue for me. After I accept Christ's redeeming work on the cross, I would be dead to sin. My life is found in Christ. Maybe it sounds simple or cliché, but I think it is true.

04.21.06

Verse: Judges 13.17-18 (NIV): "Then Manoah inquired of the angel of the LORD, 'What is your name, so that we may honor you when your word comes true?' He replied, 'Why do you ask my name? It is beyond understanding.'"

Application: I think this interaction is baller. Manoah's question is interesting, I guess (why would he really need his name?), but the angel's response is smoother than silk. NKJV says it is "wonderful." New Living Translation says, "You wouldn't understand it if I told you." The Message says, "You wouldn't understand – it's sheer wonder." KJV calls it "secret." I don't know which if any of these are correct. But I like the thought of there being something so simple, like a name, and yet it is "beyond our understanding." I think it shows the magnitude and depth of God and his angels. And how we humans will never get it. Not that there's anything wrong with that…

04.22.06

Verse: Romans 8.6 (NKJV): "For to be carnally minded is death, but to be spiritually minded is life and peace."

Application: This verse seems like it snuck up on me. I love it. It's like I've never even noticed how sweet it is. Only that can't be true, since it was highlighted in my Bible, but still. This world means nothing. We should not waste our time thinking about this world and what it can offer us. We should be spiritually minded. Worried about the souls of others and our life's service to Christ. Because in the words of Sir Charles, "Anything less would be uncivilized." (Maybe that quote was forced, but I liked it.)

04.24.06

Verse: Romans 9.21 (NKJV): "Does not the potter have power over the clay, from the same lump to make one vessel for honor and another for dishonor?"
Application: This lays it out quite simply: God is sovereign. What else is there to argue about?

Chapter 3

∞

LIGHTHOUSE MISSION TRIP TO INDIA

I am not ashamed of the gospel, because it is the power of God
for the salvation of everyone who believes;
ROMANS 1:16A

TAYLOR *University sponsors teams of undergraduate students who travel to countries around the world to spread the "good news" of the Gospel of Jesus Christ. Brad was among a group of 20 students who went to India in January, 2005. The students were asked to prepare two "messages" to share publically as they travelled from place to place. These are the two messages found on his computer three years later.*

On Doubt
Taylor University India Lighthouse Mission Trip
January 2005

Someone once asked the famous atheist Bertrand Russell an interesting question. "What would you do, Mr. Russell, if after you die, you open your eyes and find yourself in front of the great throne of heaven with God staring at you? You would know that your life's work—trying to convince others that God did not exist—had been in vain. Your whole life had been a waste. What would you do?" Bertrand Russell was not troubled by the question. He replied honestly: "I would look at God and would have a simple reply: Not enough evidence!"

It was not long ago that I was introduced to a different, yet similar, line of questioning. I was sharing a meal with my sister, my brother, and my brother's wife. My brother posed a question to us all: "What if you die to-

48

night, and nothing happens? There is no heaven. There is no hell. There is no God. There is no nothing. You die and it's over." My sister replied immediately: "I've definitely thought about that before." My response was the opposite. I had never conceived of such an option. I had never been through a traditional conversion. I had grown up with the knowledge of God, of sin and forgiveness, of Jesus. What if all that wasn't true???? No, I certainly never thought of such a thing. Of course, it's true, I told myself. How could it not be? Since that night, I have thought of my brother's question. What if?

What if it was all a lie? What if there never was a creation? What if Jesus was all man and no God? I was doing something all of us have done. Or if you haven't yet, you will one day: I was doubting. So what did I do? I did the only thing I knew I could do. I told God what I was going through. Yes, I talked with the very God I was in the process of doubting. And his answer was clear and concise: "you are not alone," He said. "Go ahead and look." So I did. I went to the Word and found something I never realized: <u>Everyone</u> doubts. Its part of being human. In Genesis 17, God tells Abraham. "You will be the father of many nations. It does not matter that you are 100 years old and your wife, Sarah, is 90. It will be done!" How did Abraham respond? He laughed. "No, no, you must be mistaken. I am…100 years old." Some people are critical of Abraham's response, wondering how Abraham could question the Almighty God. I look at his response and I appreciate his honesty, even if it was doubting. The burning bush talks to Moses, tells him exactly what he wants. This is the voice of God. Yet, how did Moses respond: "There must be some mistake, God. Who am I? Why would you want me?" Later, God tells Moses, go to pharaoh and get my people out of there. Moses, again, "But Lord you couldn't possibly want me to go. I stutter; I have faltering lips." How can you not appreciate the honesty in Moses' doubt? The book of Judges tells us about Gideon. "Surely, you don't want me to save Israel", Gideon thought. "Here, God, prove it to me with this fleece". Twice. So God did.

God knows doubt and he knows how to deal with it when His people have it. Remember Jesus in the Garden of Gethsemane? "Father, if it is possible, may this cup be taken from me." Doesn't it remind you of a little boy pleading with his father: "But are you sure, Daddy?" What a beautiful picture of the real relationship that existed between God, the Father, and Jesus, the Son.

These stories, along with other things, led me to the feet of the throne of God. I do not have all the answers. In fact, I have no more answers than that night when my brother first posed the question to me: "What if?" But, instead of letting my doubt linger inside me and building up a wall between me and the Lord, I presented myself to Him and asked for help. Proverbs 3 says, "Lean not on your own understanding. In all your ways, acknowledge Him." That's what I was doing. I was leaning on my own understanding. It gets you nowhere. But if you go to Him, even if He's the one you doubt, He will respond. Pray the prayer of the man in Mark, chapter 9. "Please heal my son, Jesus. He is possessed by a demon." Jesus asked if the man believed that He was able to heal the boy. The man responded, revealing his honesty. "I do believe, Lord. Help me overcome my unbelief."

I prayed that prayer. And the Lord answered me. "I do believe, Lord. Help me overcome my unbelief."

∽

Jesus Loves Me
Taylor University India Lighthouse Mission Trip
January, 2005

Jesus loves me. That's what I'd like to talk to you about today—Jesus Christ. Never before and never since has such a revolutionary figure existed. Jesus turned his friends' and family's lives around. Jesus changed everything about faith and religion. Jesus turned the world upside down with his words, his life, and his death. Never before, and never since, has such a commanding presence existed. Jesus had the attention of the beggars and the sick, the tax collector and the lawyers, the kings and the governors. <u>Everyone</u> knew about him. Never before and never since has such a great friend been treated so poorly by those who claimed to be his friends. One of his closest fiends, Peter, told others 3 times that he didn't know who Jesus was because he was embarrassed that he knew him. One week after a crowd of people cheered his entry into their city and shouted "Hosanna" to Him; the same crowd jeered Jesus and yelled to have Him crucified. And maybe worst of all, another one of his closest friends, Judas, betrayed Jesus for 40 pieces of silver.

JESUS. That name can stir up so many feelings inside so many people. I'd like to read you something the apostle Paul wrote in the book of Philippians.

"Your attitude should be the same as that of Christ Jesus:
Who, being in very nature God, did not consider equality with God something to be grasped, but made himself nothing, taking the very nature of a servant, being made in human likeness. And being found in appearance as a man, he humbled himself and became obedient to death—even death on a cross! Therefore God exalted him to the highest place and gave him the name that is above every name, that at the name of Jesus every knee should bow, in heaven and on earth and under the earth, and every tongue confess that Jesus Christ is Lord, to the glory of God the Father."
Philippians 2:5-11

Let's talk about that a little. The passage starts out "Jesus, who being in very nature God." <u>Never</u> remove God from Jesus. Jesus is God. The Bible reminds us that by Jesus, "all things were created: things in heaven and on earth, visible and invisible....all things were created by Jesus and for Jesus" (Col 1:16). <u>Never</u> remove God from Jesus!!!! However, this becomes harder to understand once you read the next part of the verse in Philippians 2. Although he was "in very nature God, Jesus did not consider equality with God something to be grasped." Can you imagine the president of a big company—the biggest company in the world—one day deciding that instead of being the boss of everybody, he was going to be the janitor? He would scrub the toilets and clean the floors and do all the dirty work. Well, Jesus was king of this whole universe, and one day he decided that he was going to step down and serve not as an angel, not as a ruler, not as a king, but as a lowly and unsung human. Then Philippians continues: "Jesus made himself nothing, taking the very likeness of a servant, being made in human likeness." Jesus was the ultimate servant. Less than a week before he was going to die, Jesus committed the ultimate act of service. Surrounded by his 12 closest friends while he was on this earth, Jesus got down on his hands and knees, he took off his friends' sandals and he washed their feet. Do you guys get that? This is the Lord of creation, the maker of the universe, and he was washing the feet of his friends. (PAUSE) "Being found in appearance as a man, he humbled himself and became obedient to death—even death on a cross!" Let me ask you guys a question? Who here is looking forward to dying!?!?! Probably not too many people, right? I know I'm not. Well, Jesus wasn't either. Especially a death as painful as he knew he was about to experience. He would have thorns crushed on his head, nails driven through his hands and feet, and an angry crowd yelling at him for the whole thing. Yet Jesus did it. (PAUSE) He went through all of that. Why? Because he loved you. Jesus loved you. Jesus loved you. "God exalted Jesus to the highest place and gave him the name of Jesus that every knee should bow in heaven and on earth and under the earth and every tongue confess that Jesus Christ is Lord, to the glory of God the Father."

If you know what Jesus did for you and you want to feel His love for you personally, go to Him. Ask Him for life. And He will give it to you. Jesus will give you life fully.

God is Crazy
A message Brad gave at the Upper Peninsula Bible Camp
July, 2005

I want to start by saying something that may startle you, but I will do my best to clarify what I mean in the next couple of minutes. So here it goes: our God is crazy! It was about three weeks ago that all of us summer staffers were being led in a time of praise and worship by Ms. Lisa VanRyn, which as you know is really a blessing. We sang a song which contained a line that stuck out to me. When I approached Lisa following the singing to thank her, we talked for a minute or two and she mentioned that exact line from that same song and how it had stuck out to her as well. The song is called "Indescribable." The line goes like this, "You see the depths of my heart and you love me the same." Since that night, I have thought about that fact many times and I have come to a conclusion. That is the same truth which I startled you with a minute ago--our God is crazy. He is crazy about us. His love for you and me is so inexplicable and unbelievable. He sees the depths of my heart and he loves me the same? Are you kidding? The depths of my heart contain some truly disgusting things. I mean, I am a despicable person. I was reminded of my own depravity. This morning at Chapel you heard the message that faulty thinking is an attempt to rely on your own righteousness. In the words of Deuteronomy 9, we are stiff-necked, corrupt, rebellious, and wicked. And yet—in some divine miracle—God's love remains unfazed. The 103rd Psalm reminds us of that in verse 12 reads, "As far is the east is from the west, so far has he removed our transgressions from us." I was thinking about David writing that Psalm, I thought, "couldn't he have just said, 'as far as the earth is from the moon?'" but nope, that wouldn't have worked. He chose two things that will never ever meet—"as far as the east is from the west, so far he has removed our transgressions from us." Our God is crazy. Verse 11 says, "for as high as the heavens are above the earth so great is his love for those who fear him." Once again, David chose a distance that is indefinable and unfathomable. "As high as the heavens are above the earth, so great is his love." Our God is crazy. If you bring to him a broken and contrite heart, he is quick to forgive; a concept which is so tough for us lowly humans to conceive. He is probably the only one who can truthfully say, "I have forgiven you and I've forgotten what you even did." He sees the depths of our hearts and he loves us the same. Our God is crazy!

As part of the India mission trip experience, the students were required to keep a journal of their thoughts and experiences leading up to, during and following the trip. This "additional" journaling by Brad provided some unique insights and reflections into his life at that time.

12/18/04

And so my journal begins, at least the journal that I am writing for this India trip. In reality, I have kept a journal since the first day of the New Year during my junior year of high school. Whoa, that was 4 years ago?!?! Time literally amazes me. It seriously seems like it was just a week ago when I was in Mrs. Haugh's homeroom and that was 6th grade. I remember jokes I told, reasons I got in trouble, and presentations I gave. And that was almost a decade ago. A decade ago. Are you kidding me? I am getting old I tell you. Tomorrow I will wake up and I'll be 40 with a mortgage and car with an engine that stutters when the wind chill dips below twenty.

1/11/05

...to fulfill my journal requirements, I am supposed to write about stuff that I would never write about by choice. For instance, I am to "make connections between what I have studied and am now experiencing." I cannot do that very effectively because none of the study I studied impacted me very significantly... moving on, here is something: "Do I feel comfortable relating to the nationals?" I will answer a "no" to that one. Usually I feel awkward, like I am clearly trying to force interaction. I fumble over words which makes our language barrier quite convenient for me. I feel like I am alone on this one too. Most everyone on the team is a lovely communicator, pushing over language barrier as though they were Reggie White or Warren Sapp in a Peewee football game. And then I come in, "Duh duh what's duh your duh name duh?" I feel like an idiot because I know how terrible I am at it. I'm like the president of the chess club asking the prom queen if she wants to double-straw a chocolate milkshake with me. Of course, she always has better things to do. I would, too, if I were her.

1/13/05

…Now for another journal reflection: "What are you learning about God's global purposes and your role within them?" That's a good one. I really do appreciate the fact of the global church and our brothers and sisters abroad. I think the mission of the global church is the same as my church back home. And that is two fold: 1.) minister to those already in the body and 2.) bring more into the body. I am not really sure what my role is within that yet. I doubt I will know it by the end of this trip, too. I need to know/experience/grow more before that is decided.

1/19/05

…now we are in the home stretch of the trip. It is just lovely knowing that the people back home are thinking of me and praying for me. It's a special thing, it is. I am guessing you journal readers want me to open up a little more—maybe reveal a little bit of my heart, as the learned sages say. "What has God been doing to me?" Well, he's been showing me how big He is. I'm not sure how great it is, if it's great at all, that we have satellites and astronauts taking pictures of the world and passing them out to classrooms and putting them on the back of the sports section with weather formation patterns on top of it. Sure, it's great from some perspectives—educationally and all that. But something it has done in my subconscious is miniaturizing the world. Maybe it got me thinking that this place isn't so grand after all. We make bouncy balls and pencil sharpeners into globes these days. What if we didn't have any of that? What if we were always fully aware of how really big this place is? What if a figure like 6 billion people actually meant something? I guess I am just appreciating that a little more through this trip. God is the God of Elm Grove,

Wisconsin. He is the God of 13510 Braemar Drive. He is the God of Taylor University. And Indiana. And the Midwest. And the United States. And Vellore. And Bangalore. God is the God of the universe. India, USA, Earth, all of it is His.

…Also, our journal guidelines really stress us talking about missions and missionaries. This is not something I would normally talk about but here are my thoughts: I have crazy, mad respect for missionaries, Aretha Franklin style. These are people who have fully and unabashedly given themselves wholly to Christ. It's an awesome thing. It's easy for a doctor or a business man or most occupations to not think about Christ one day or one week or maybe even a month. Maybe nobody would notice a change in them at all. But I think it's next to impossible for a missionary to forget about Christ. He is so central to their everyday interaction. Their life is Christ. That is what I love about them. That is what I look up to in them. They are so sold out for Christ. I admire that.

Part II

THE REST OF HIS STORY

And let us consider how we may spur one another on toward love and good deeds.
Let us not give up meeting together as some are in the habit of doing, but let us
encourage one another and all the more as you see the Day approaching.
HEBREWS 10: 24, 25

Chapter 4

∽

BRAD'S DIARY: HIGH SCHOOL ENTRIES

I want to document these things because if I don't I will forget them and this is a very special time in my life that I don't want to forget.

BRAD LARSON

∽

B RAD *started his diary on September 6, 2000 at the beginning of his junior year of high school. Initially, the entries were very simple, consisting of a few words that appear to be prayer notes about family, friends, exams he was taking, or events at school or church. Regardless, there were a couple of notable entries that first year, which are transcribed below as written:*

∽

12/25/00
    What I am thankful for this year:
    -family—mom, dad, Jeff, Dawn, Grammy
    -friends-Yord, Bruce, Melv, Nate Bogs, Jake, Jamie M., Jamie H., Dana, Kumer
    -role models—Nelson, Aalsma, Malvig, Torrenga, Vance, DAD
    -Heritage
    -The Word, The Son, The Father, The H.S.
    -All blessings I've been given that I am stupid enough to forget

1/1/01

2001
New Year's Resolutions

-Think about what I say before I say it
-Don't feel dumb, at all
-Write in journal every day
-Miss quiet time <u>only</u> once a week
-Get a girl, for goodness sakes
-Talk more to Mom and Dad
-Maintain a Bible study
-Don't put people down, esp. those I don't know
-Watch what I think about
-Tell Mom + Dad I love them more
-Be strong in opinions, but be willing to change them

1/1/01

Dear Book,

What's goin' on? Yesterday was pretty fun. It ended what was probably the funnest and best year to date. First off, our JV basketball season was the best thing I've ever experienced. I had too much fun. I looked forward to practicing every day. Games were the best. Next I made a lot of great friends. Nate Boggs and Jake Anderson are probably my best friends right now. We have so much fun together. My other new friends are Jamie Miller, Dana Pietrangelo, and Jamie Hishmeh. We all hang out all the time and have so much fun . I worked at Boston Store this summer and made $2500. Pretty solid. Got in an accident which sucked. Read the Bible and prayed a lot more. Which is sweet. Still teaching Sunday School with the Brucer. I like it better this year. Again, this year was money.

3-6-01

...I went out to Uno's w/ Yord, Mom and Lynn (*Hawkins*). We had to talk about a college trip. I told Mom the only schools I want to see are Wheaton and Northwestern. And that I would never go to Taylor...

3-8-01

...after school I went to Southridge (*Mall*) with Jake and Aalz. We walked around, with me and Aalz continually reminding each other of the "31" Club. Sweet, huh? I also told them how I was thinking last night. I am so blessed and all I do is complain. From now on, I'm focusing on what I have and not what I don't. The Lord has given me so much and what do I do? Throw it in his face and ask for more. Enough of that, man. Later after dinner I went to the Milwaukee Rescue Mission w/ Mom + Dad to listen to a message. The homeless guys there make me count my blessings. "What a Friend We Have in Jesus."

3-19-01

Today was sweet. School went well...I gave hugs to a bunch of guys today-Jake, Aalz, Joel, Strom, Drout, Melv. Just happy to see 'em. I love those guys. I was just embracing life today. It was fun...

3/20/01

Today was fun, till the last 5 minutes. The day was fun. I just had a good time all day. Just embracin' life as Jake and I like to say. Got kicked out of Drafting Class but that's okay. After school, I came home to go to Disc Go Round to sell my rap and some other stuff. Then I went to Best Buy and bought a VCR so I can fall asleep to my ballin' (*basketball*) videos. After that I went to the sports banquet. Came home and told Dad I got a VCR and he went nuts. He thinks I am gonna watch porn on it or something. He doesn't know I'm in the 31 Club.

3/21/01

...Life is so much better when you're positive...came home and had a talk with Dad and Mom about the VCR. He's not worried about me, he just wants me to spend more time with them, which is fine.

5-12-01

Dawn woke me at 12:30. (She was home for Mother's Day). Anyway, my gift to Mom was supposed to be our lunch at Uno's. But she wouldn't let me pay. She said it meant more to her that I would ask for us 3 to go out to lunch...Praise God for Mommies.

9/11/01

Today was probably the worst day in the history of America. At 7:45 and again about 8:03, 2 hijacked commercial airliners flew directly into the World Trade Center. They collapsed about an hour later. Then the Pentagon got attacked by another. Thousands of people were killed. Watching the second plane fly into the side of the WTC was probably the scariest thing I have ever seen. Then people had to jump from 100 floors up to escape the flames. 266 people on 4 flights died. Then I realized that my Uncle Charles works in the Pentagon. After Dad got word to me that Mom (who was flying to Houston to attend Nancy's funeral) had landed safely in Tulsa. She is driving home right now. Charles is safe but he was in the Pentagon when the plane crashed into it. Mr. Moore scared me pretty bad when he told us, "Boys, I'd be afraid if I were you." Nothing will happen I'm sure but the day was still quite freaky. This just made me realize how trivial all my "problems" are. God is good.

10/7/01

.....P.S. I think I forgot to mention that Mom and Dad had a minor purchase the other day: a new house. They, on the spur-of-the-moment, bought a cottage on Enterprise Lake, 3 hours north. What a couple of psychos, hey?

11/5/01

Now if BT *(Brent Torrenga, a favorite high school teacher)* ain't one of the best guys in the world, I don't know who is...when BT was introducing me he said something about me being bad at Frisbee. Whatever, I didn't even pay any attention to it, right? So I get home about 9:30, BT calls me to apologize in case he had offended me. I told him I hadn't even thought about it. Either way, though, what a guy. I think him and Dad are the 2 people I most want to be like. Maybe sneak Jeff *(brother)* and Mike Perso *(high school upperclassman)* in there too. What a guy!

∞

THE *remainder of the entries of 2001 relates conversations and events that oc-curred between Brad and his friends. Many of the entries were detailed conver-sations of classroom events, basketball games in which he played, or his contact with girls that he liked from afar, never really directly sharing his feelings to them personally. He also saved, within the pages of the spiral bound notebook containing the diary, cards and letters of encouragement that he received from his Mom. Throughout the diary there are the typical insecurities expressed that we have all experienced as a teenager, but there were no "secret sins" and there was certainly an acknowledgment of God and prayer in his writings.*

∞

THE *"We the People" constitutional law competition between high schools is held annually across the nation. Local and state-wide events lead to a state winner who proceeds to a national competition between all fifty states, which is held in the spring in Washington, DC. The "We the People" teams from Heritage Christian High School in Milwaukee, Wisconsin, the school all of our children attended, has prepared diligently for this event for fifteen years. A Heritage faculty member, Mr. Tim Moore, regularly pushed his students in this competition to achieve goals they would never have thought possible. Heritage Christian was the frequent Wisconsin champion over the fifteen year history of the competition in Wisconsin, but they had never placed nationally in the top ten. This year was to be different! In Brad's diary entries, we can see how Mr. Moore motivated his students so that they could realize the fruits of their efforts. While Brad and some school friends were working on the "We the People" proj-ect, he offered this observation:*

1/13/02

"Today was long. I got up at 8:15AM for first church service. At 1 PM, Liz and Tim (*Brad, Liz Culver, and Tim Cisler comprised Unit II of the "We the People" competition.*) came over until 7:45 PM. No, it's not a misprint!

We finished our question 1 responses…..Mom was wonderful yet again. She brought us juice and made us those chicken biscuit things. They were telling me how much they love my Mom. I do, too."

1/18/02

I headed down to Mr. Moore's room for our final dry run. But before that started, he praised us ridiculously. "I am truly humbled by you guys in Unit II. This is the reason teachers teach, for times like this when your students amaze you." He told me specifically how good my writing is and how precise I am. I know from Jeff that the last day he would praise you to boost your confidence but I didn't expect that. Before all the other stuff, he says, "I don't usually talk from my heart…" Dang.

1/20/02

So, yesterday was amazing. We met at school and rode the minibus to Madison *(for the state competition)*. I studied the whole time. Everyone met in this huge congressional room before each group split off into our respective rooms. Ours was packed with students and tons of parents. Kind of intimidating. And Unit II starts it off. Of course our worst question (about the Electoral College) was first. Well we didn't let that stop us. We were money. I cited the Yale Law Journal, Liz got Lord Bryce in, I got in Caleb Strong, the 1824 election, Tim was money too. We did really well. Tim said he saw Mr. Moore bust a cigar when I was talking. After, Mr. Moore said it was a good thing that Unit II started because we set the bar high. Every one was praising us. People were telling us how amazing we did and how impossible it would be to follow us. I thought we did well but I think we could definitely have done better. In his comments, Kaminski *(one of the judges)* goes, "Brad, I've been doing this 15 years and I am positive that no one has ever cited Caleb Strong." That was funny. Unit VI went next and also did really well. Mom and Grammy came for the afternoon. Unit V started us out and did really, really well, Bruce especially. I was okay. Unit III did a lot better than the AM session. Unit IV did real well. VI was really good. And then II gets to close it out. Kaminski and 2 new judges say, "We" will be doing question # 3". Sweet deal--Feds and anti-feds. We were $. I got in FDR's Executive Order

9066, Gulf of Tonkin, executive's blending. Liz and Tim were awesome but I really don't know what they said b/c I was thinking while they were talking. After it was over, Kaminski gave us the E (excellent) word. One of the other judges compared Heritage's legacy to the New York Yankees in baseball. I think that is what moved Mr. Moore to tears. After, Kludt (*a classmate*) said, "Brad is my father." Meredith and Liz—"Brad you are my hero"."How do you remember all that stuff? It is like you are reading from a book. Incredible." Liz cried. I gave her a huge hug. I was so happy and proud of what we did. Everyone was like, "Unit II is the best". So we have to wait about 45 minutes in the huge congressional room til everyone else shows up. Then the announcement came, "First second place—Greenfield HS." "Second second place—St. Joseph's." "Third second place—Wauwatosa.""Yeah!!! We won!!" I was so happy. I thanked Mom and Grammy first. Then a thousand pics. A "high five" from Mr. Moore.....yesterday was sweet.

Over the ensuing weeks, the "We the People" groups prepared for the national competition which occurred in early May.

Saturday 5/3/02

What a weekend, man! One of the greatest of my life with my to-this-point biggest accomplishments ever…So we arrive at the airport on Friday at 7AM. We lay over.....we got into DC about 12:30…the team had a meeting in Mr. Moore's room at 9:30PM. "You guys know this stuff. You have no reason to be nervous. Trust yourselves. Calm down. You'll be fine." We met as a unit for about an hour and a half or so.

5/4/02

Got up at 7 and nervous as h*ll… the day starts and I guess you know who started it off—Unit II of course. We were $. We were really good. The judges liked us. Team effort…Mr. Moore came up to us and, "I heard the E bird (excellent). Great job. I wouldn't rather have any other Unit lead us off." "6 for 6." Moore says. Everyone was really happy the rest of the day. That night we had a meeting, "Just go out there and do your thing. Great job today."

Sunday 5/9/02

On Sunday we don't go until 4 PM. For some reason I am not so nervous, but I should have been....Unit II starts off again and we get smoked... but Moore comes up and tells us that the judge asked tough questions because he knew we were tough. Sitting next to Liz must have done something to me because we were both bawling....but all the other groups did a great job. There was a dance that night and at 9:15 they announced the Top 10. The guy does his introduction and then busts out, " and in no particular order, the first group to be walking up Capitol Hill tomorrow is.... WISCONSIN!" Yeah!! It was crazy. Everyone is screaming and hugging and no one hears the next 6 or 7 teams. "You know how sweet this is that we did this for Mr. Moore," says Kludt. We do pics for a long time. I call Dad and Mom and Jeff. It was so awesome. Its turns out that for the first 2 days we were 6th of 51 states.

Monday 5/10/02

We got up at 8:30AM and leave for the Senator Dirksen Building. When it was our turn the other units did well, some better than others... and then 2 hours after our group started, Unit II is up at 11:30AM. We all did great. # 2 deliberation question. I got in my Patrick Henry quote, Liz her "had every Athenian been a Socrates" and Tim's quote about "Is a saw a good tool?" comment. Mr. Moore then gave us a nice speech: "Take a look around..." He said that we had a really tough judge and a really bad lady disguised as a grandma, but we did a great job....after walking around that afternoon we went back to change for the formal awards dinner that night. After dinner there were some regional awards and the greatest 15-20 minutes of my life. First, the announcement of seven 4th place teams. We all hold hands and Liz tells me that if we get in the top 3, she's gonna kiss our cheeks." "In no particular order, the first 4th place team is....Virginia!" Then another state and another state with the excitement building each time. The fourth, 4th place team is their first time in the top 10...oh, man... well it had to come to an end some time..."New Mexico!" We're still alive. Fifth—Colorado. Again a popular top 3 pick. "And the sixth, 4th place team is.....California!" I stand up and inadvertently blurt out an expletive. Oh, sh*t!", but only loud enough for Liz to hear, thankfully. That was

Liz's and my favorite moment, I think. "You just swore in front of your Mom" she whispered. I was amazed, Mr. Moore predicted California to win it. "And the seventh, 4th place team is....................Texas!" Oh, my goodness! We couldn't believe it. We did it. They announced 3rd next... WISCONSIN!" Hugs all around. I looked at Liz and she almost cried. I looked back at Mom and went to hug her. We got a sweet plaque after a long walk thru the tables that sat 1500 people. They announced the top two winners and then Liz dragged me out on the dance floor and everyone got their groove on. We went back to the hotel and I called Jeff, he was so pumped for us!..Mr. Moore told Liz that Unit II was "the heart and soul of this team."

Tuesday 5/7/02

...we flew home and were pleasantly greeted by a lot of people. Parents, friends, teachers..more pics..more hugs...then home. Mom said it "was the coolest thing any of my kids has ever done." But I knew you wouldn't know how cool it was unless you were there. Then bed. What a weekend. P.S. I love Liz and Tim.

Wednesday 5/8/02

Mr. Moore's speech last nite stressed 2 things: "A mind, once stretched, never returns to its original shape. And, how he loves that we take risks."

BRAD *really loved high school, but it was not until he was in college that he reflected on those memories:*

12/29/03

The boys convinced me to go practice basketball at HSC *(Heritage Christian High School)*. It was actually really fun. I was thinking a bunch today about high school and how much fun it was. If I could, I would re-live it, I think. I think about it more than the average person, because I liked it so much. I loved basketball, I loved carelessness, I loved laughing with Kumer. I feel bad when people talk about how much high school sucked 'cause they must have missed out on something. I always think of the casualness of your basic school day: driving to school listening to the radio, uncalled for comments toward the teacher that made people laugh, the bell ringing to dismiss us, lunch, being bored in class, and, of course, practice after school. How could I not enjoy that?

Chapter 5

∞

THE COLLEGE EXPERIENCE

And let us consider how we may spur one another toward love
and good deeds...let us encourage one another—
and all the more as you see the Day approaching.
HEBREWS 10:24, 25B

ALTHOUGH *Brad was raised in a Christian home, attended church weekly,*
taught Sunday School to junior high school boys for three years, and at-
tended a Christian school from fifth grade through high school, it was at Taylor
University in Upland, Indiana where Brad grew spiritually and socially. At
Taylor, he found himself in an environment that challenged and nurtured both
the academic and spiritual potential of his young mind.

The students are required to sign a Life Together Covenant (LTC) in which
they committed to abstain from alcohol and tobacco during the school year.
Also, chapel services and certain aspects of Christian behavior are expected
of students attending such an institution. But the strength and eternal value
of Taylor University is found in both the faculty and the students themselves.
Drawing students from most states and many foreign countries, each class has
about five hundred students, equally divided by gender. Most of the students
live and eat on campus. In contrast to many other universities, the dormitories
are separated by gender, but mixed by class, so that on any single floor there are
freshmen, sophomores, juniors, and even seniors. Such was the third floor of the
east wing (3rd East) of Wengatz Hall, Brad's floor for four years.

It was on 3rd East Wengatz that he bonded academically, socially and spiri-
*tually with a very special group of men. He was both spiritually challenged **by***
*and challenging **to** his peers. He was befriended by upper classmen as a fresh-*
man and later vice-versa. He was introduced to a deeper level of Bible study

69

than he had known. It was here that he wrote in his journal, maintained his diary, and conducted his prayer life. But it was also here that he had just plain fun. The Men of 3rd East Wengatz argued for hours over nonsensical things (i.e. do you get wetter walking through the rain or running through the rain?) and more serious matters (i.e. is there time in heaven?); they played pranks on each other, and grew to love college life in every sense of the word. Brad made many references to the men of 3rd East in his diary, as you will note in these excerpts.

The First Days at Taylor University

7/12-13/02 (*Orientation weekend at Taylor*)

We picked up Yord (*Hawkins*) + Lynn (*Hawkins*) at 8:30 AM + drove down to T.U. We got there, registered, took ID photos, listened to a talk, ate, and shook too many hands. I was having my doubts so I prayed. Then during a Taylor Today skit, there was a line—"The day really rotted." I burst out laughing + couldn't stop. So that lightened my spirits. Then a neato ice cream social. After, I met 3 dudes from our wing—Ben Harrison, Preston, and Taylor. Real cool, funny dudes. I was happy. Me + Yord were the only frosh there…I had a time figuring our whether I was 3 East or 3 West.

8/29-30/02

So I'm here. We left at 8:15 w/ Dad in the cargo van. We had a nice drive. Good talks w/ good tunes. Got here around 2 + set up stuff til 6. After dinner, we met our probe groups. My leader is a female named Drew. She's pretty nice. Then we had a Wengatz hall meeting + a wing meeting. About 10:45 or so, our wing went to Steak 'n' Shake w/ our sister wing 1st East (*Olson*). I drove with some nice girls. I got there + sat in a totally random seat. Somehow, it was next to this amazing chick—Shelby something. I just let her talk. Man, I didn't know if she was talking about puppy dogs or how hard it is to talk to her dad, I just nod my head + crinkle my eyebrows and somehow, at the end of the night, I turn out to be a big sweetie…

∞

IT *is obvious that Brad did not like Taylor University in the first few days, but that quickly changed. His adaptation to Taylor and college life was important enough for him to include it in his testimony two years later:*

"...My first week of college was tough for me. I didn't like the bed I would be sleeping on for the next year. I didn't like being away from my parents. I didn't like the fact that I was growing up. After about a week, God came to me. He reassured me more than anyone I knew could. He told me, "I have everything under control. Don't worry about anything. You're going to be fine." And of course, He was right. I quickly made friends, I actually enjoyed the classes I was taking, and I got so over my homesickness that I barely even wanted to come home on the holidays when I had to..."

∞

BUT *it was tough that first two weeks, as noted in this abbreviated series of diary entries:*

9/1-2/02

College sucks. I really hate it here. Some of the guys are nice enough but it is not fun. Yesterday we went to chapel with our sister floor, then to lunch. It's real boring during the day....tried to change my schedule but I didn't want to wait in a three hour line...so I've watched a "Law and Order" marathon all day. I hate it here.

9/2-3/02

...yesterday night, I went to Ivanhoe's a local ice cream shop with some dudes and a few girls. There, we laughed about our parents crying when they left. Got up at 8 and changed my classes. Had a frosh orientation class at 10. Then a discussion group for a class I haven't even had yet. At 1, I had a US History class. Then I called and emailed people and said how much I hated this. This prompted Jeff (*Brad's brother*) to call and give me a pep talk. Then an ice cream social and back to the dorms to chill and do nothing.

9/4/02

Dawn (*Brad's sister who was a junior at Taylor at the time*) called and she came over and we talked. She's praying for me.

9/5-8/02

I don't remember much from Thursday. On Friday, I had to go to this stupid pick-a-date with this chick I had never met. We ate at the Dining Commons, then bowled, then I had to watch <u>The Rookie</u> outside on the wet grass just so I could politely say, "Thank you."

9/8/02

....tonight was real fun. First, we gathered in Luke Lentscher's room and started discussing the pick-a-date 3 weeks away. I mentioned my dream girl, Shelby, which initiated a phone call to her to find out if she dates only Bible majors. She wasn't even there but it was real fun discussing it with the guys.

9/9-12/02

All these last few days blended into one. Two nights ago we watched <u>The Count of Monte Cristo</u> in Jake's room. Tonight was real fun. About 5, I went with Dawn to see <u>City By the Sea</u>. It wasn't too good but it was nice being with Dawn. At 10 or so, we ambushed the girls who we thought were ambushing us earlier in our shaving cream fight that was scheduled for 10:30PM. It was real fun. Mark taught us how to burn down our cream shooters so they would shoot farther and it worked real well. Also, Shelby recognized me despite the fact that I was covered in shaving cream. I am so money, baby!!

9/13-16/02

This weekend was real fun. We had our wing retreat up at Luke Lentscher's in Waupun (*WI*). I left w/ Yord, Yordy, Luke L., Nate

Hoekenga, John Lee, and Brett Kraftson. Six ½ hours (one of which was naked hour) later, we were there. We went to Dr. Lentscher's office and used his aqua massages, massage chairs + it was sweet. Back to his house... to hoop it up before we climbed into the giant Jacuzzi. Going to sleep that night was so funny...my favorite line of the weekend from Preston— "Goodnight Sun. Goodnight Moon. Goodnight Stars." Got up at 10 or so + spent the day on a cloudy lake with jet skis and 2 power boats. That night we had a nice devo time + lots of peeps shared. We left on Sunday around 11. I was w/ Bryan Beeh, Nate, Brad K, and David Whitney. We stopped at U Dub (*University of Wisconsin*) + Beeh's house for a meal. Met some honeys on the way back...

$$\infty$$

10/22-28/02

Highlights from the past week: us raiding the 3rd West/others campout for Airband at 4 AM w/ water balloons...; dying while seeing "Jackass" the movie; Fall Fest 2K2 at Yordy's w/ the sister wing, countless games of whoop-a** b/t me and Steedj in NBA Live 2003; a shirtless late night trip to Burger King Thursday night.

10/29-11-04/02 (*Brad's 19th Birthday*)

Ahh...the big one niner. My last year as a teen. Let's hope it's a good one. This past week was fun. On Friday, I went to "Punch Drunk Love" w/ Mark + Boyers. Alright. On Saturday, I went on the 3rd floor English pick-a-date with Ashley Rammer's roommate-Kristi. It was long, fun, + expensive: brooms, t-shirts, pizza, gas $, Pepsi Coliseum rental, + Denny's. Got home at 2:30 + had a sleepover w/ Boyers in Mark and Lentscher's room. Went to Bedside Baptist...Sunday. Today was nice. A normal day...about 10 guys went to Olive Garden—me, Yord, Lukes, Mark, Peebs, Yordy, Micah, Yet + Downey. It was fun. The hot server touched my back. And I got the birthday song. And we got asked if we were from Ball State. (Peebs response: "No. We're from Taylor. Fire up the Coke machine.") Well, it was funny then...What friends I have.

12/19/02

Ahhh.....so I survived my first semester at college. Not ½ bad, I'd say. I'll probably come through with a 4 point. Socially, not bad either. I got Boyers, Mark, and Lentsch. Still no ladies. One of the most glorious moments of the semester occurred last night at dinner. After pouring myself milk, I turn to walk to the table. And who is coming my way but only the "hottest of the hots"—M. H. We have immediate eye contact and I, of course, would have been a fool to look away. Here's the surprising part— she didn't look away either. And almost simultaneously, we throw each other half smiles. My heart leapt for an unspeakable joy. I almost dropped my tray.

5/13/03

...somehow Mark (*Van Ryn*) and I had a heart to heart. We both opened up big time—him about his past, me about my lack of past. That guy has his head on straight, a lot straighter than mine, I'll say. He's a smart dang kid and all because of one thing—his cousin's death. Talk about the Lord making a positive out of a negative. Romans 8:28 in action.

Sophomore Year at Taylor University

BRAD *continued to journal faithfully during his sophomore year. The diary entries consisted of every day experiences such as lifting weights, watching basketball games, h-dubs (homework), watching television shows such as Jeopardy and SBTB (Saved By the Bell), personal and corporate devotionals with friends, intramural sports, working in the dining hall setting up banquets for special events, and just hanging out with friends. It was in the spring semester of that year that he decided to change his style of writing.*

2/7/04

...I think I'm going to change my writing style in these notebooks. No longer will I recount classes, lifting, etc. unless something occurs worth mentioning. I will try to write only things worth recounting. I will also try to add my thoughts on various topics. Time will tell if this is the right move, but I think it is. Ten years from now, what good is it to know that I lifted on a certain day when I could have recalled my thoughts on the presidential race of 2004?

∞

In the spring of 2004, Brad, Jeff, and their Dad flew to Texas to take some golf lessons and have some "quality, guy time." The mission was accomplished. At the same time, Brad made these observations while waiting in the airport.

3/10/04

It has been on this plane flight that I have realized two things. First, man is an amazing creature. That one might have the mental capacity/imagination to think that some day huge and winged pieces of metal weighing however many tons and holding however many hundreds of peeps might transport its contents from city to city in perfectly reasonable amounts of time while soaring above the clouds. Why, I could never have conceived of such a thing had I not grown up with it. The capabilities of the human mind amaze me. The other night, I was looking at the moon. The moon, I say. To say that we, man, have been there and back is a feat which will never cease to astound and humble me. Here I am struggling mightily in retaining the espanol conjugation for the estar verb in its subjective form. And then there's man, plotting his next voyage to that illuminated celestial ball which is however many thousands of miles away from us. Certainly God has gifted us in too many ways.

My second observation: During our takeoff and subsequent landing, one in a plane witnesses those that are ground-bound in a way in which the latter is comparable in size to an ant. And, in my humble guesstamation, those humans seem to be just as busy and bustling as the ant. That brings me to my general wondering: are we fascinated by the ant for any particular reason other than its size? Are they, in fact, the hard workers that we've always imagined them to be? It seems to me they're not. But if

75

that were the case, why would the Psalmist (or was it the Proverbist) who commanded man to "look at the ant, thou sluggard!" My general wondering is surely fruitless, doing nothing for me but wasting my time and approximately half a sheet of paper.

∞

4/19/04

In Ancient History today, some things took place. We were watching this PBS video on Augustus and it was talking about his daughter Julia, who used sex as a means of gaining power. It shows probably a half dozen shots of her in bed with guys, naked and finally one in a nasty position (missionary, I think) when Mrs. Hoskins jumps up and apologizes repeatedly. The class is silent as she stumbles up to stop the video. Mike Parsons, 6'8" genius, says: "So, is that gonna be on the test?" It was fantastic!

∞

Junior Year at Taylor University

9/21/04

Here is a very random thought: I really enjoy life. Pretty much every stage I've thus entered I have liked better than the former. Now, if what Jeff says is true, then the next stage (post-college marriage) will be a bit of a let down. I think I'll be able to deal with it. At least, I hope so. But for now, everyday has its own reasons to rise out of bed. I really just like being alive, experiencing things. It's a pretty sweet gig, this thing called life.

9/22/04

Tonight, we had our first small group—me, Steedj, Gladly, Bergman, Celby, all lead by our fearless leader—one Marc "Raul", if you will, Belcastro. I am excited. Marc should be a great leader. I hope this role gives me the opportunity to open myself more spiritually—to him specifically. I already

76

appreciate his friendship so much and I hope that this will only add to that. I have high hopes.

9/28/04

But then for my bright part of the day—I talked to Marky. That boy is a genius. I love him with every fiber of my being. He brightens my downtrodden spirits as no other can. Don't worry, my spirits were not downtrodden but I wanted to use the word, anyway.

10/18/04

The Spanish oral exam/questioning period was much easier than expected. All that worrying for naught. I suppose all worrying meets with the same fate (Matt. 6, baby!). Today was a day when life was enjoyed. For some reason, at dinner I had this amazing and somewhat indescribable feeling that all is well with the world. Most of that had left me by the time Lighthouse class was started.

10/26/04

Since I forgot to tell you what happened in Intro to Philosophy last Thursday, I will pretend as though it happened today. Somehow, we were talking about tumors and how disgusting and disturbing they are—eating you alive, capable of destroying your body, growing hair and teeth (no joke). Spiegel likened tumors to a spiritual metaphor of what sin can do in our lives. How destructive something like a drug addiction or pornography addiction can be, all we (the victim) do is nurture and care for it and invite it to consume us. All we really need to do is ask for the power of God to destroy it. Also during Spiegel's descriptive explanation of how nauseating a tumor actually is, our class had what I felt to be a bonding moment. No one held back their laughter, especially our fearless leader whose merriment sounded as though it exceeded all of ours. I looked round the room and no smile could be repressed. It was a beautiful thing. And this, from a class where I could count, using only my phalanges, the words I have spoken to anyone this whole semester.

10/27/04

Raul and I discussed a female prez today at lunch—the possibility of one, the benefits and drawbacks, etc. I believe it a possibility but hold back on labeling it a good thing. He holds back on both things, believing a black Prez to be more likely than a female. Time will tell.

11/08/04

...at 11:11 PM the event of the year occurred: Club 336, owned by Grant Chapman and Zimmy Jimmerman and bounced by one Celby Hadley opened up. Sheer delight and rootbeer flowing, guys in club attire, pimp lighting, tunes jamming. It was heaven for about 23 minutes. Honestly, the best thing this year. Inexplicable times of merry making.

11/09/04

Today, the men of 3 E reflected on Club 336. And we all (by we all, I mean me) got down on our knees (by our knees, I mean my knees) and thanked the heavens for the geniuses who inhabit that oh-so special abode. Dr. John Stott spoke tonight. He was, in short, genius.

11/14/04

Now, I assure you: I set two alarm clocks last nite, as I usually do. I checked it twice. One of them was away from my bed, which would require a prompt exit from my slumbering state to turn off the painfully annoying beeping. They were both set for 7:55. I awoke at 8:50, with both alarms off. And it was too late for church since I had to work at 10:15. After dinner tonight, I enjoyed a priceless one hour stretch with Zan, Weston, and Ahern. We watched movie previews, talked about Zan selecting "small" when given the option of small, medium, or large, as in the size of trailer. It was one of those inexplicably beautiful scenes which transcend space and time (despite it being an hour) and contain in it the enigma wrapped in a riddle that is Third East.

11/30/04

Today was a purely lovely day. Not for any reason in particular. At dinner tonite, we talked about passing people on the sidewalk: whether or not we support, have we ever been passed, unconscious pace changes, etc. It was enlightening. Tonight, Justin spoke to Third East about self-control. I thought he was awesome. He just got me, for lack of a better term, fired up to serve God. He showed the redemption clip from Les Miserables and I had to hold back the tears. Then at 12:30 tonight, we celebrated muy capitan's birthday with your basic bathroom power outage, followed by excessive celebration.

12/22/04

My bum hood is reaching new and unexplored levels. My highs today came from exchanging emails on ineptitude with A., which is highly enjoyable. Jeff and I encountered several problems picking up food tonight. First of all, he spent 15 minutes at a Chinese food place, leaving me sitting on a cold, steel bench. And we could not find the right biscuits at the grocery store. All that before dividing our forces for the checkout lane. He chooses the express line, waiting behind about 5 people. I chose a line behind a couple. However, my fault was not noticing that they were clearly preparing for Y2K5. Either that or they were foster parents for two dozen needy children.

12/28/04

I love my brother. I never really expound on him, I realize. So I shall now. He is quite possibly, the funniest person I know. I probably throw that title out there too often, but he is at least in the top 10. He says things that are incredibly witty. Even his off color comments seem to have a slight charm to them. I agree with him that he is the best when he is around Becky. He says jokes that I could never dream to make, yet he maintains lovability with it. Granddad died today and we are all at peace with this.

4/7/05

Tonight, we had a baller small group. Actually, it is always baller. No joke, whenever we meet, I walk away sharpened, enlightened, encouraged, and lots of other good things. It was just Raul, me, and D. tonight. We covered a day in My Utmost (for His Highest) and then got into sin and the moral life. D. told us about his pastor's downfall. It is amazing the things that sin can do to someone's life.

Finally, one of the events that brought the school year to a close is documented in this entry:

5/18/05

Best night of the year! Definitely a contender, and its not even close to over yet...Tonight, after wing pizza at 9:45, the seniors exited the lounge in order to prepare a special gift to us: naked wing slip 'n' slid. Boyers brought a huge sheet of plastic and then blazed it with laundry detergent and a little water. What unfolded next had life-changing power. Bodies colliding, genitals smashing, eyes burning action. We would slide so far. Westie slid all the way into 3 Center. Unforgettable. Even Moose and Klav got in on it. Absolutely amazing. And in 11 minutes, Club 336 will sponsor yet another event: Bubbly Bonanza, to take place in the showers of 3 E. Cannot wait...

On my! Better than I could have imagined. Of course, we were decked out in 3 E outfits—thongs and the like + gather in the halls in the minutes before 11:11. When the minute hand finally reached the 11 mark, we stormed in, seniors first, followed by those who will be gone next semester. We were instructed to douse ourselves in laundry detergent as we entered. Why?, you ask. I thought everyone knew that it glows under black lighting. 336 plastered on the walls, we busted open our bubbly. After most was gone, there was awkward silence b/c the music in the hallway wasn't reaching the shower. But that inspired us—make our own music! Rapping, chanting, football cheering, 3E and 336 praises being shouted. It was so glorious. I cannot describe the happiness we all were experiencing. Lentscher came in + dumped the entire trash can of detergent on his face. Apparently, my eyes and face made me look like the Anti-Christ b/c they were glowing so much from the detergent. I have to say, this probably topped Club 336. Maybe. It's at the very least arguable. Wow, that was so hotness. I love tonight so much.

Yet another addition. We used the chains from someone's super lift and locked up Yog's door to Rossa's (*door*). Then we opened up Yog's window thru Grant's and chucked in an airhorn with the trigger duct-taped down.

We quickly evacuated to our respective rooms and pretended to be sleeping. To provoke him further, Boyers phoned his room several times and hung up. He finally got out and yelled down our sacred hallway, consumed w/ anger, malice, and rage. He deserved such a lesson in anger management, and he failed.

Chapter 6

∞

THE 12/3 INCIDENT

"Brad said he did not regret his actions of that night and boy did we have fun!"

KYLE "STITCH" LANTZ, A 3RD EAST WENGATZ WING MATE

AND FELLOW PARTICIPANT

DURING *the late evening/early morning hours of December 2/3, 2004, an event occurred in Brad's life at Taylor University which would have a profound impact on his view of the world and his relationships with others. Little did he, or his parents, realize its significance and the consequences that followed. What began as a seemingly "harmless" prank by some overly energetic college students resulted in a special mentoring relationship with a much respected philosophy professor at Taylor University.*

∞

12/2/04

This night will go down in Taylor history…About 12 o'clock I went to the Apt and almost missed one of the greatest nights in the history of Taylor. I made it back literally 2 minutes before a previously unannounced naked run. Emails had been sent to all students this week telling of a scheduled power outage that would occur between the hours of 1 AM and 5AM. Someone on 3 East had the genius to realize that this presented a picture perfect opportunity for a naked run right through the campus. So the power goes and we storm down the stairs and de-clothe ourselves in some trees. Our first stop was the bell tower; keep in mind the campus is only illuminated by the moon. That is what prevented us from seeing the couple we passed during that stretch and we nearly ran right into them. Then, our crowning achievement: we, 15-20 nudees, ran through the galleria. We passed one female inside before congregating in the entry way closest to Wengetz while we contemplated where to go next. Then a female voice invades the area from the doorway 10 feet away: "Hello, this is a girl." We all go crazy and run back to the bushes where we started. But that didn't stop B.B. from walking right up to the girl, thinking it was his sister (!??!) and saying, "Becky, it's me." That is when he realized that it was not Becky. When we get back to the dorm, the campus began their fun. And by fun, I mean mostly idiocy. First of all people (roughly 200) gathered at the Nativity scene. When Campus Safety pulled up to spotlight it, some joker ran at him and slid across the hood of his car. Campus Safety was powerless. He just sat there making sure no one stole a wise man or anything. Suddenly, someone yells, "Fire!" and the whole crowd runs over towards the front of Olson Hall where some idiot had started to make a nice sized bonfire (!); some people are not so smart *(in the words of Kevin Welty)*. This inspired some morons on Second East to yell obscenities not worth mentioning out the window. That is when I decided to go back outside. Eventually, Campus Safety came over to the fire which effectively moved the group back to the Nativity where now people were climbing on the camels and stealing the shepards. Maintenance showed up moving the crowd in front of the Wengatz side of the library. Then the Upland Police and Fire Department vehicles show up, probably only making things worse. They couldn't do anything to 200 people. That is when I came back inside and pretty much all had died down roughly a half hour later...The campus is now abuzz with rumors, which is not good for anyone. So be it.

12/3/04

This place was gossip city all day...the whole night we talked about what was going on at the mandatory all-campus meeting that the President called through an email at 5 PM. We were already out the door and missed it.

12/5/04

...I confessed with the others to our dormitory supervisor of my "transgressions" and also to my parents who took it surprisingly well.

(We remember this phone call very well. Brad made sure we were both on the phone and then told us of his nude run, along with others of 3rd East, a few nights before. Although we initially thought it was funny, Brad was perfectly serious that this was "not a laughing matter" and there would be serious consequences. We told him of our support for him and wished him well in his discipline.)

12/07/04

Well, tonight we had our disciplinary meeting. It went far, far worse than expected. When I got back at 7:00 to change for the banquet, they told me what happened to B: expelled for one year. So all of us were nervous. We all gathered at Rupp 203. That is where I started to get quite nervous—heart pumping, adrenaline rushing, pits sweating. The 6 administration representatives arrived at about 7:25—they then explained what would be happening—all individual meetings, then decision, then they tell us what was happening. I met with the associate dean and the campus pastor. I thought my meeting when quite well. Randy called me both "bro" and "man". I just explained what went down, basically moment by moment. Then we all gathered outside the chapel for what seemed like an eternity and compared with each other how our meetings went. They finally called us up to the Stuart Room. The dean of students preached to us of what he called "sexual deviance." And about the emotional trauma to girls on campus. Then the news: suspension for J-term, disciplinary probation, and a project, yet to be determined. People were in shock, I think that means that L and A cannot graduate on time. And A. and I cannot go on the Lighthouse trip. I called Mom and Dad right away. I have no idea how to describe their reaction. They were sorry for me. Not angry. I don't know. The hallways were filled till 2 AM discussing it.

12/8-9/04

The last 2 days have been a whirlwind. My mind was not able to focus on anything but this. I emailed my Lighthouse Mission team last night— told them what I did and what's happened since then and told them how sorry I was. The amount of encouragement I received was incredible. I have been so lifted up. I got a little teary, both writing my Lighthouse email and then receiving the responses. We had a wing "prayer and share" session at 5 PM today and I thought it was awesome. Chacko touched my heart and made me want to cry. This really brought us together. We have received notes from Olson Dorm—anonymous people telling us how much they looked up to our honesty and integrity (which we clearly don't deserve). It has just been awesome. Then my Lighthouse meeting tonite was unbelievable. How much people care and sympathize and love me despite what I did. The team prayed for me for about 20 minutes and I was so moved. I can't describe how encouraged I was having been through this. This is the Lord bringing good from an impossible thing. I am so grateful for how our meetings went.

The following is excerpted from a letter from the Dean of Students outlining his punishment, which included the following disciplinary sanctions:

12/9/04

1. You are suspended from attending the J-term Lighthouse Mission trip to India. (*This meant that Brad had to return the money to friends and family he had raised to support his trip to India, a very embarrassing admission.*)

2. You are placed on Disciplinary Probation effective until the end of the spring 2005 semester, which is the most serious status into which a student is placed prior to dismissal.

3. You will write a three page essay focused on what you have learned as a result of your participation in these behaviors and the impact that your behaviors have had on your spiritual journey and how these behaviors negatively impact the Taylor University community.

4. You will inform your parents of this incident and the resulting disciplinary sanctions.

5. You will meet with a faculty mentor, approved by the Dean of Students, on a weekly basis from now until the end of the Spring 2005 semester

Thankfully, within a few days, a reprieve was given by the administration, based on letters and requests from fellow students, who were very supportive. Brad would be permitted to go to India. He continues in his diary:

12/13/04

India, baby, I am so in. Yes, you heard it here first. Our alternative punishment: disciplinary stays, limited use of car for 5 weeks, 40 hours of community service, 3-5 group meetings with the Dean of Students and best of all—a curfew—10PM on weekends and 12 on weekends until Spring break (7 weeks). I don't even care. India is back, baby! Everyone on my team was crazy pumped. It was baller. This whole thing has been incredible.

One of the requirements of the "reprieve" stated, "You will meet with a faculty mentor, approved by the Dean of Students, on a weekly basis from now until the end of the Spring 2005 semester." Brad chose one of his favorite teachers, Dr. Jim Spiegel, a professor of philosophy, to be his mentor. These scheduled interactions over that semester came to be very special for both Brad and his mentor, as can be appreciated in Brad's diary entries and in the letter that Dr. Spiegel wrote Jeff in the days following Brad's death. Brad referred to Dr. Spiegel with a variety of terms including "Spieg-easy" and "genius".

2/20/05

I attended vespers and upon running into Spiegel (who was speaking), I said to him, "There he is...the man, the myth, and the legend." His lackluster reaction reminded me that I don't really have a substantive relationship with that m/m/l *(man, myth, legend)*. So I felt like a fool. But still his talk lived up to his reputation. He has sick game *(this is meant to be complimentary)*. His words inspired an interesting convo among three of us *(Raul, Ahern)* about treasures in heaven. I am not really sure what I think about it.

3/15/05

Met with Spiegel for the first time today. What a sick baller. We talked about that night (12/3). He remembered Jeff from 3 or 4 years ago. He talked about modesty. Just a straight-laced, straight-faced no-limit baller (*a term of respect and endearment*).

3/23/05

I met with Spieg-easy today. We chatted about the things spoken of during his session with us last week. We got into how important it is to be open about sex for the kiddies. He also talked about how unoriginal it was to streak. He told me "in strictest confidence" the pranks he had been involved in. (They were impressively creative, but hardly drove me to tears of humor.) He was more concerned about the lack of creativity than anything. I asked him about fasting. He emphasized being aware of pride and engaging also in secrecy along with it. Denying yourself is such an important discipline. He told me about his own family and growing up and some of the mistakes that he had made. But by 22, he was very morally serious, even though he wasn't a serious person, he said. He's just baller is what it just comes down to.

4/5/05

I had my 3rd and best meeting yet with Spieg-easy today. He shared with me the plans for his next book....it sounds as though it will be a genius piece of work. Naturally. He also told me about his hero, a philosophy professor in college. After thinking about it, he decided to follow the advice of his youth director (advice he originally scoffed at, but now agrees with): "Find someone who you want to be like, and be like them." So here it is. I then introduced the idea I have been kicking around lately: the moral life makes sense. Even if I found out God didn't exist, I doubt my lifestyle would change. I wouldn't want to cheat or lie or drink or be promiscuous. It is so much easier to not be those things. What seems like the harder decision at first becomes the far easier path. He told me something his father-in-law told him: "The way of the transgressor is hard." Or as Mama Spiegel apparently reminded her son: "Men will throw away their entire lives for a few seconds of pleasure." Just think about it. Of course it's not worth it to sleep around or "try" drugs or pick up smoking or have one more drink. It's easier not to. I like that. One more quote from today, more relating to the earlier point: "Change one life and you've changed the world".

4/14/05

I met with Spiegel today. We talked about movies at first; I asked him how he decided what to watch. He and his wife make choices based upon critical acclaim and recommendations. I wasn't completely satisfied with his answer, to be honest. Talked about time management. I asked him about addressing God in different ways and what he thought about that.

4/21/05

I met with Spiegel yet again today. He told me he thinks his son will look like me someday. Baller, eh? We talked of parenting. He thinks we insult kids by giving them sing along tapes to listen to. His kids listen to U2, the Smoking Popes (?), David Bowie, etc. His oldest is 5½.

4/28/05

Spiegel is an absolutely filthy individual (*this is intended as a compliment*). He possesses knowledge beyond limits and restraints, unfounded in this world and possibly grounded in the next. (That does make sense). He explained today that if you wear WWJD bracelets or have an ichthus on your vehicle, you better be constantly aware that you're putting yourself on display, saying, "This is what Christians do." He praised Aalsma (*Brad's high school mentor*) after I told him that he had refused to put a fish on his car because he knew he would be judged. If you are going to do it, that's fine; you just need to understand what it means. He told me his thoughts on traffic laws, saying, "The law is not simply what the street sign says but how it is interpreted by those who enforce it". He compared it to an umpire in baseball—calling strikes as he sees fit and not just how the strike zone is strictly defined. He says cops pull over people who dangerously ignore the flow of traffic, even if it is 5 or 10 miles per hour over the limit. Go with the flow and you will be safe and a good driver in the cops' eyes. I've never heard that view, but I like it so far. Today was our last meeting (tears fall to page). He's too busy for me, apparently, I understand though.

HERE *is an email from Jeff, shortly after returning from the Memorial Service for those who died in the April 26, 2006 accident.*

Mom and Dad--here is an exchange I had with Dr. Spiegel. JDL

-----Original Message-----
From: Jeff Larson
Sent: Monday, May 08, 2006 4:25 PM
To: Spiegel, Jim
Subject: BJL

Dr. Spiegel

I believe the last time we talked was a few years ago, before I graduated in 2002, when I asked you if you would be willing to write me a letter of recommendation for medical school. I regret that I am not writing you under better circumstances.

My family and I got back to Milwaukee today from the memorial service last night for the students killed last week. The service was memorable and touching; we are so grateful for the love and support we have received from the Taylor community.

I am writing you to let you know how much Brad and I have looked up to you. You were one of my favorite professors, and when Brad started college, I told him that you were one of the best professors I had had at Taylor and that he had to take as many of your classes as he could. Thankfully, he heeded my advice.

Here is a funny story. I remember when he was disciplined for the incident now known only as "12-3," he told me that as part of his punishment he had to choose a faculty mentor and that he had chosen you. I was jealous. I told him that when he got together with you he should ask you if you remembered having me in class. Brad said, "Dude, he is never going to remember you. Do you know how many students he has?" I agreed with him. After your first meeting, he called me and told me that one of the first things you said to him was, "So you're Jeff's brother." I'm sure you don't remember this, but it made my day.

I want you to know how much he loved his time with you. For him and I both, it was so refreshing to know someone that was simultaneously wise, smart and funny. I think the real blessing was knowing a Christian who had an open mind and who had well-thought opinions that were a lot different than our parents. I don't know much about the content of your interaction. Brad and I had a couple conversations about it, and he said only that your talks were great. I wish I could have eavesdropped on them. He emailed me many of your papers and articles. We had a great time discussing them. He referred to you as "the man, the myth, the legend," so that might give you an inkling of how highly he thought of you. I hope you find some humor in that.

I feel privileged to have known Brad and to have been his brother. He was such a special kid. I loved talking to him, especially in the last year or so. Maybe you can appreciate this: I really thought he was in his intellectual wheelhouse. He was at that special time in his life when he was reading a lot, he had established some key spiritual principles, and he had an open mind. There wasn't anything he wouldn't read or opinion he wouldn't listen to. I loved that about him. He and I had such a good time talking and bouncing ideas off each other. I think that is one of the things I will miss most: his mind. And whether you realize it or not, you were instrumental in this process. For that, I am grateful to you. I apologize for my thoughts being poorly organized, and I am also sorry that parts of this email have been about me. I would have liked to have told you some of these things in person, but I guess this will have to do. I just want you to know how much you meant to Brad and how much I have continued to look up to you through him. I am disappointed that

God's will had Brad dying when he did. I don't understand it, but I am doing my best to trust it.

Take care and please give my best to your family.

Sincerely,
Jeff Larson

"Spiegel, Jim" wrote:

Subject: RE: BJL
Date: Tue, 9 May 2006 10:15:36 -0400
From: "Spiegel, Jim"
To: "Jeff Larson"

Jeff,

Thank you so much for taking the time to send me that encouraging letter. I must admit that it took me a while to get through it, because of the tears... I attended the memorial service Sunday night and was much impressed by the faith of all the friends and family members who shared, including your dad. It's hard to imagine more tangible proof of the eternal hope we enjoy in Christ. I actually do recall making the connection that you were Brad's brother and being glad to see that there was a good streak of critical thinking running through your family.

I am so glad to hear that I had some sort of positive impact on Brad. I consider my task as a professor and writer AND as a husband and father is to fortify Christian souls. Any feedback confirming that I'm having some success in this is edifying, but under the present circumstances it is most humbling and encouraging.

Coincidentally, I have been intending to contact your family to share my impressions of Brad, particularly during our private "mentor" meetings last spring. I recall how in my Intro class in fall 2004 Brad did such excellent work but said almost nothing in class. It was one of those classic cases of "still waters run deep." Every question or comment he did make was very substantive and showed how thoughtful he was. By the end of the year when we began meeting as a result of the "12-3" incident I could see that he had "ripened" in his quest for wisdom and understanding. So it really couldn't have come at a better time. The first thing we did was go over his part in the events of that night. I was impressed at how Brad was so willing to accept responsibility and to learn as much as he could from the experience. In fact, he showed more remorse for his comparatively minor role in the events of that night than did many of the ringleaders. And it occurred to me that Taylor needed more students with that kind of character--a humble willingness to confess, repent, and learn as a result of their mistakes.

From there we discussed SO many things, from philosophy to theology, to family to popular culture. It really was wide-ranging, and he was like a sponge, both intellectually and spiritually. As you say, Brad was in his "intellectual wheelhouse" and I suspect that this only continued over the course of the last year, though I didn't have much contact with him.

The main theme or focus of our talks, of course, was moral-spiritual in nature. We discussed the virtues and what it means to have integrity and a Christian character. I was deeply impressed by Brad's earnestness and moral seriousness--far beyond even most Christian guys the same age. As we chatted, I kept thinking, "This is how I want my sons to be when they are 21 years old" and "This is the kind of young man I want my daughter to marry some day." Brad will always remain a fixture in my mind in this regard. One of my first thoughts after hearing that Brad was one of the four who died in the crash was how well-prepared he was to go. All of our discussions of virtue and the spiritual disciplines, and his spiritual growth that followed, were, in a sense, preparing him for his departure two weeks ago. I see our lives here on earth as essentially a time of preparation for the true reality of our eternal existence with Christ and the community of his saints (see 1 Tim. 4:8). Brad grasped this at an uncommonly young age, and his life beautifully showed it.

You, and especially, your parents are to be commended for training and encouraging Brad in his Christian faith. The fruits of this faithful service are being demonstrated right now in Paradise. And through Brad your parents have inspired me in my own parenting. So count me, my wife, and kids among the throngs who have been blessed through the faithfulness of the Larson family. Thanks again for writing and please know that your family remains in my prayers.
Jim Spiegel

P.S. Please share this note with your parents (and anyone else, for that matter).

Jeff, Dawn and Brad on Brad's 21st birthday

Brad and his Dad

Brad on a vacation with Dawn, Jeff and his wife, Becky

Brad with his parents and Dawn in Oxford, England

The men of Third East Wengatz in a light moment.

A railroad trestle near Taylor University tagged by Brad's friends shortly
after the accident: Third East Wengatz loves BJL

The Memorial Prayer Chapel at Taylor University

"Brad's Bridge" spans a gully from Wengatz Hall
to the Memorial Prayer Chapel

Many of the Third East Wengatz men returned to Taylor for the dedication of Memorial Prayer Chapel on April 26, 2008

Charlotte Marie, Jeff and Becky's daughter, reaches out to Uncle Brad

Chapter 7

∽

THE OXFORD FILES

THE *fall semester of his senior year, Brad was accepted into a study abroad program through Taylor University. This gave him a unique opportunity to study at Oxford University in England, where he took courses in The American Revolution and Constitution (from the British point of view), C.S. Lewis in Context, etc. More importantly, the experience allowed Brad to extend himself "beyond his comfort zone", as his Mother had been encouraging him to do since high school. We have chosen to include all of Brad's diary entries, as they reflect his insights, humor, and personal discipline as he adapts to a culture foreign to Taylor University.*

In Brad's application to study at Oxford he provided this response to the question of the basis of his faith:

In what ways might your faith influence how you approach your major area of study and in what ways would your major area of study inform your faith (500 words)?

My faith has a profound impact upon my study of History for several reasons. First, I approach History knowing there is a magnificent Creator God behind everything that has taken place throughout time. Without Him, man is nothing; man has no existence and is without history. "I have made the earth, and created man upon it: I, even my hands, have stretched out the heavens, and all their host have I commanded." (Isaiah 45.12). Second, I have the knowledge that all things have a purpose. Nothing happens that God does not see. Throughout all Scripture, one sees God's wonderful plan unfold; that process continues today. "The Lord of hosts hath sworn, saying, surely as I have thought, so shall it come to pass; and as I have purposed, so shall it stand" (Isaiah 14.24). A final way that my faith influences my study of History is found in the knowledge that through all the events of history, God deserves the glory. My faith allows me to understand that all that happens was fore-ordained by the Maker of the universe, and His design deserves glory. As Paul wrote, "For of him, and through him, and to him, are all things: to whom be glory for ever" (Romans 11.36).

Similarly, my study of the field of History has deeply influenced my personal faith. Could there be a more analytical method to learn more about the heavenly Father than by studying His created beings that have walked the earth before me? Some of the ways that History enables me to gain a deeper understanding of the One that guides me are by studying the path of God's chosen people, the growth of the Church, and the rise and fall of empires and leaders who have shaped the lives of all who follow them. In addition, History affords me an appreciation of the special relationship God has to His created beings. This godly relationship can be seen from the earliest Biblical characters of Adam, Noah, and the patriarchs through the thousands of years of written human history to the figures of today, in the twenty-first century. I understand the privilege I have to study history like no generation has before me. Because of the innovations and recent advancements of technology, man has access to an unimaginable amount of material, especially when considering the resources of just a decade ago. History, like its Author, is a subject that has no bounds. It has no end and an often-disputed beginning. One thing remains certain: my short-time as a historian has deepened my faith and matured my life as a Christian.

Bradley J. Larson

As part of the application process, Brad was also asked to comment on how he would maintain the commitment not to drink alcohol, smoke or engage in activity unbecoming to a Christian student he had made upon entering Taylor University.

Bradley J. Larson
September 28, 2004
LTC Commitment Essay

I have never had a problem abiding by the Life Together Covenant that Taylor has its students sign every year. I have seen the mistakes of others in regards to some of the things that it restricts, and the Lord has allowed me to learn my lessons through their experiences, instead of discovering them for myself.

I am not attracted to nor can I envision myself participating in the actions that the LTC disallows – drinking alcohol, sexual promiscuity, dancing, and smoking, among others. I would doubt that my feelings toward those practices would change with the atmosphere of a new college. This is despite the fact that much of the socializing in a place like Oxford can be done at the local pubs. Through talking with others who have participated in the same program, it is totally socially acceptable to go to a pub and just order a soda. Hopefully, I can be a witness to those who may abuse the practice of drinking alcohol by drinking it for the purpose of intoxication. If asked, I will explain the commitment I made at my home university and what it means. Being in the age group that I am, in the culture in which I was raised, it is not an uncommon occurrence for me to be in situations where alcohol is present. But I constantly remind myself of the command of Ephesians 5.18: "Do not get drunk on wine, which leads to debauchery. Instead, be filled with the Spirit."

It is my prayer that the Lord will give me the strength to resist temptation as I enter into a new place with unforeseen enticements. I trust that He will be faithful to that request.

∽

September 1-2, 2005; Thursday - Friday
And so I have arrived, with relatively few complications. I left my mum and sis at roughly 8 pm Thursday evening and have been all by my lone-

some since I traversed my way into this establishment they call Crick Road. When finally arriving in Oxford courtesy of the bus system, I met several other SSO participants, including my roommate. His name: Matthew Gillikin, a philosophy major senior from Covenant College. He is definitely an interesting cat, and so far, I have nothing but positive feelings for him. I feel as though everything he does has the potential to be unintentionally funny. A couple hours after I met him, I was trying to picture him in my head and I couldn't stop from altering mental images of Bryan Beeh and then Ty Humphries, so I will say that he is a hybrid of the two (in aesthetics alone). I like him. We took a taxicab to Crick Road, where we met Jonathan, our "junior dean," who I would describe as our babysitter but he is probably more like a hall director meets resident assistant. There are twenty-two of us living in this joint and forty or so in The Vines (the other student residence), all Americans. Matthew and I quickly met our third roomie upon arriving – Anthony Campau. Nice guy and very normal looking. He is a senior at Southeastern College in Florida, although he resides in Michigan. He also seems to be a bit of the opposite of a homebody, as he has already spent a semester in DC and a summer in Mexico. He seems to possess an intimidating genius, a fact that makes me feel somewhat impotent in his presence. Jonathan seems to be a good feller; he has been a student here at Oxford for over ten years, "which must be some kind of record," he joked. Of course, his accent is very strong, but that is only part of the reason that he reminds me of Hugh Grant. He also possesses the flimsy body frame, the floppy hair, and the classy British wit slash charm. He uses very words like "brilliant" and "nifty", and lambasted one kid's attempt at calling the "garden" out back a "backyard." And everything he says sounds very intelligent, thanks again to his accent. Anyways, my bags did arrive tonight while I napped off some of the jet lag, but I should be recovered by now. That might be all I have to report.

Highlight of the night: I return from the bathroom and say something to this effect: "I don't know how much I'll be doing laundry this semester," because we'd been told both the washer and dryer will cost two pounds a piece. Matthew immediately responds, "Yeah, I'm gonna smell awful. I'm never doing laundry." I like his honesty.

September 3, 2005; Saturday

The action in the day didn't really start until about 3 pm, when we began our journey to the other student housing location called the Vines, about a thirty-minute walk for us. This was a walk after which I sang praises upon high that I will not have to complete everyday, as our house is less than ten minutes from the city centre (Ya like that? I've already got the British spelling thing going on. I am so sweet. I always knew I was sweet.) So we arrived and there are definitely advantages to that establishment. There are twice as many kids, and most of them are smarter, better looking, wittier, and more spiritual than anyone here. Also, their "garden" (again, notice my sweetness as I employ the Jonathan-ordained term for "backyard") is gigantic, and we quickly realized it would be quite suitable for wiffle-ball. Now, those who know me probably realize that my sweetness does not extend into the realm of the fielding sports, but you'd be surprised at what a guy like me can do when pitted against some of the notably intellectually gifted from the small, private Christian college community that seems to extend across that great nation of yours. (I say yours because, of course, I determined that I am now a Brit, which means I'm superior to you in every way.) Now, I thought I had maxed out my baseball-ish abilities as a second-year fourth-grader playing back-up right fielder for the Town of Brookfield Phillies, but it seems as though I am surprising myself lately. Let's just say this quickly, so the tooting of my own horn is more like a modest rustle: I went 2 for 3 with a couple doubles and had some truly awesome one-handed grabs of that tiny, yellow, holey sphere. See, now I know that you are impressed and I'll do my best not to let that taint the way I write the rest of this entry (man, my newly realized sweetness is already infiltrating my genius). Following the double-header (yes, we played two tonight), a few of us headed to the Eagle and Child, of course the famous hangout of those two writers of those famous fantasy series that everyone seems to be digging lately. (I don't care too much for fantasy myself, but whatever floats your boat, I guess.) Anyways, those two jokers used to hang out across the street, too, at a little local joint they call the Lamb and ___?___ (*Flag*). Unfortunately, the latter of the two random objects that seem to adorn all local pubs is escaping me at the moment. But what is with that name business? We passed another one called the Angel and Greyhound. And I think I heard they were putting in another place called the Ferret and Staples. Apparently, all you have to have to get a piece of property here is a name consisting of either an animal and/or a heavenly being, along with the most random thing you can think of in your last night of sobriety before your new bar opens. But, anyways, my first full day was splendid. Look at all I've accomplished – not sleeping in, reading, tearing the other team up as though they were a piece of unrolled cigarette paper in wiffle-ball, watching other people drink at one of Oxford's choicest pubs, and all this before the clock struck midnight. And, in case you've already forgotten – I discovered the true essence of how sweet I am.

September 4, 2005; Sunday

I got up later than planned today, but still, I was ready to conquer the tasks of the day. First off, my roomies and I went to the grocery store. I felt quite accomplished following that menial task. Spending just seventeen pounds, it seemed to me like I got a pretty baller deal. I probably got jacked, but no sleep will be lost over it. Anyway, this afternoon, I walked alone to the local University Park. I tell you, it is straight out of Finding Neverland. I half expected to stroll right past Johnny Depp daydreaming about dancing bears. But alas, I did not. The trees in this park are truly amazing. I am jealous that we don't have something like them in the states. There is this one that looks kind of like a giant bush and if you look closely, you see a tiny doorway into the middle of the tree's base, protected from the outside world by its branches. It was incredible. The parks are incredibly well groomed – freshly cut, very green, little trash. And you just see people lying out on blankets enjoying themselves. It is a beautiful thing. I spent about two hours there, taking in the sights and reading a little bit. Truly enjoyable. I came back just before teatime started, an event for the entire student group hosted by our house. I met and chatted with Grace, a girl from Cali who goes to school in British Columbia, and Nathan, a bearded fellow from Alabama. I enjoyed listening to both of them very much. Both have seriously considered becoming Catholic and may still do so. Very intriguing people. This evening, we went to an Anglican evening church service. It was not what I expected. The dress was very casual, as in wear anything you please. The worship was contemporary, as in Here I Am to Worship. The message was very oriented to the specific church itself – St. Andrews, it was called. I didn't think it was entirely applicable to the Christian life anywhere. We ended with the Eucharist, which of course, although I hadn't considered it yet, featured real wine. Ironically, it was the first time I have taken it with real wine. I was startled and wondered if I should feel bad (about the Life Together Contract). Then I remembered I was taking the Lord's blood and scolded myself for degrading it with meaningless worries.

September 5, 2005; Monday

So basically, I have been severely dehydrated since my arrival. I can remember urinating a total of three times since hitting Heathrow. Either I have a really bad memory or my tummy is craving more liquids. The thing is, I rarely feel thirsty. But when that stream of yellow before bed is a scarily neon shade of yellow, your body is telling you that there is a problem. Anyway, I think today we must have walked a total of anywhere from fourteen to forty-seven miles across Oxford throughout the late morning and afternoon. And you know what the sweet thing about it all was? I forgot my camera. So I had that goin' for me, which was nice. We began our orientating today. We met the Director of the program and all his meager henchmen and women. But I am unnecessarily degrading them for the benefit of the reader; in reality, they are kind, God-fearing souls. We had our tour of Oxford, which included some truly interesting facts that my brain didn't think necessary to record, unfortunately. I do remember C.S. Lewis being mentioned, and Handel's Messiah, and the Director's daughter Adeline. Unfortunately, the relevancy of those persons (and their respective symphonies) was not carried along with their names. We ended our afternoon of education by having a cup of hot tea (Who thinks to end a grueling, sweat-inducing tour by sucking back some scalding hot flavored water in a three and half ounce cup that has a handle built for an infant? The British, that's who!), and watching the first part of a mini-series on the History of Britannia. Quite a day! I have been eating quite poorly of late, and I anticipate this becoming a bit of a habit. Don't worry; eating poorly doesn't mean I have been munching Gobstoppers and sucking on a two liter of Dew. Poorly means PB&J-rich and nutrient-deprived. We'll see how that goes.

September 6, 2005; Tuesday

Today, we met much of the staff of Wycliffe Hall and had a tour of the joint. Wycliffe Hall, for those of you wondering, is the college that I will be studying at this semester. Oxford University is a conglomeration of either thirty-nine or forty colleges under the umbrella of Oxford. You may have heard of Christ's Church College or Queen's College. Now, if you were wondering where my school is on the University's totem pole, Wycliffe Hall will not be challenging Christ's Church to a game of cricket anytime soon, since we only first became an official college in 1996. But hey, if I was in the NBA, I wouldn't complain about playing for the Clippers, either. Our building is named after the great and celebrated John Wycliffe. Don't recognize the name? Well, then I would be busy questioning my salvation if I were you. John Wycliffe was the first man to attempt to translate the entire Bible into English. And oh yeah, he was martyred for his faith. Take this dude seriously. He is not to be messed with. Neither is the staff of his Hall, including the little dude that serves our tea every afternoon promptly at 3.30 (which is actually 15.30 here. Who knew that the Brits would live by Army time?). Anyway, I am effectively intimidated by the workload and material. But I have come to the conclusion that even if I get an F percent, they can't take away my family and friends! I love you, guys. (Shout out to my moms! Much love, much respect, Moms!) And the assurance of all of your reciprocating love is what keeps me going through this academic gauntlet. Anyways, I'll give you three guesses as to what I had for dinner. Nutrients? No. Vitamins? No, but getting closer. PB&J? You got it. And that was accompanied by three eggs, which may or may not have been way too underdone. (What is with that mucus-like ring next to the yellow part?) Enough for today.

September 7, 2005; Wednesday

Today, we had lectures a plenty. I found part of one of them (there were four) to be actually, quite fascinating. And to make that even more impressive, it was regarding the (what I thought to be) incredibly dull topic of medieval cartography. We talked about these prehistoric maps called T-O maps, so named because their globes features an O-orb shaped- globe with its main land features (Asia in the North, Europe in the Southwest,

106

and Africa in the Southeast) forming a T shape. Like I said, surprisingly interesting when the lecture was accompanied by corresponding pictures. (I am such a child of the late twentieth century. I disgust myself.) We finally got our University cards today, which will serve as our proof to all doubters and nay-sayers that we are, indeed, Oxford students. My main accomplishment today was relieving my nerves about book renting at the Bodleian Library, something I have feared since my arrival. It was a confusing process, but one that I am certifiably glad I now know how (that's a lot of "ow" endings right in a row... wow. There's two more!) to do. I don't know where all my time in the day goes. I don't feel like I waste time, but apparently it all goes someplace – the Netherworld, perhaps. Here it is, 12.16 (actually 00.16), and I have no idea where this night went. I bought an airline ticket tonight for our end of September break. I will go to Rome with my roomie Matt and two dudes – Owen and David. It cost them 60 bucks at eight o'clock tonight and it cost me 80 bucks at 12. Marx wasn't kidding when he said that money moves at the speed of time. Or was that MasterCard?

September 8, 2005; Thursday

The mornings here are pretty consistent. I start by getting up and hopping in the shower (which is quite tolerable, after a subhuman experience in there the first day). This may sound like your first ten minutes of any ol' day, too, but this is where things change. I then select my outfit for the day, doing my best to "fit in" (i.e. not wearing my Proud to Be an American tee or my Don't Mess with Texas bandana). Unfortunately, I usually fail miserably in my search for neutral tees, as I possess an obscene amount of t-shirts that feature the name of an American city – such as Milwaukee, for instance. Today, I chose a Bob Dylan t-shirt I have, making me basically as inconspicuous as I can hope to be here, given my lack of options. Getting back to my morning routine - I then make my way downstairs to our community kitchen and take special care in pouring a bowl of cereal and perhaps a yogurt, if I feel a desire for some thick dairy product. Consumption of said product(s) follows. Mmmmm. Some people don't eat breakfast; what in the name of the starry heavens above are they thinking? They are depriving themselves of one of God's greatest gifts to humankind – that of energy! After brushing my toofers, I make a casual stroll to Wycliffe Hall, where I am greeted by sixty-one of my closest friends (i.e. my fellow SSO students) and our stand-in mothers, fathers, brothers, sisters, and god-nieces (i.e. the Wycliffe staff). Life is good. We begin our days with an hour-long segment in the History of Britain video series that I have mentioned in previous entries. It's actually quite fascinating. Today covered the revolutionaries of the late 13th and early 14th century – William Wallace, Robert the Bruce, and the like. You Americans know these men as Mel Gibson, the pitiful wannabe Scottish king who betrayed Mel Gibson, and others, all of whom bear some semblance of a relationship to Mr. Gibson. Tea follows. I have no taste for tea, and have little interest in acquiring one. So what follows for me could more accurately be described as watching others drinking tea, which is always a blast. The way they hold the cup and look like a bunch of fairies, taking minute sips every three to four minutes, making that disgusting slurping noise. People are fascinating. We then return to the lecture area, where, ironically, lecture follows. We have had a range of topics – everything from Oxford's architecture to the roots of Anglo-Saxon literature to the Augustinian approach to knowledge. Most are good, but some have been rough. Two lectures, then lunch (featuring some variety of meat product), another lecture, and then something to mix it up, usually. Today, it was a short field trip around Oxford. We saw the Oxford castle, which has a tower that has been standing since the year 1004. Then, we went to Christ's Church, which is quite breathtaking. We saw John Locke's tomb and this amazing stained glass window known as the Jonah window. But more importantly, we saw the steps of the dining hall at Hogwart's Academy. For those of you know-nothings out there who are clueless, you need to wake up to The Real World. And by the real world, I mean the ever-changing and multi-faceted world of J.K. Rowling, the immortal genius who has penned the book series that has changed my life and my sense of reality – Harry Potter. Please, if you haven't yet, make the plunge into her enchanting and mesmerizing world of ghosts and goblins, witches and warm-blooded princes, minions of the Evil One and devilish sycophants. You won't regret the jump. We were then free to roam. Freely roaming one of the most fascinating cities in the world? Is this a joke? Am I here? Me and a dude I know (he'll soon gain "buddy" status, most likely) hit a pub tonight and just mucked it up with the locals over a brew. Who am I kidding? In reality, we sat alone at a corner in the back and I got a Coke (with lemon, mind you). It was still more baller than should be legal. (In case you hadn't heard, Congress is actually debating some baller legislation on the Hill come November, after the elections; you understand the bureaucracy, right?) This place is ridiculous. And so are you – for reading this whole thing. Who the H-E- double hockey sticks do I think I am, asking you to read this semi-worthless summary of my day, intermixed with my thoughts on nothing and then some. The nerve of some people will drive me loony someday...

September 9, 2005; Friday

Today could be considered incredible. We had a day long field trip to one of the oldest cities in all of the United Kingdom, just north of London. It is called St. Alban's but was formerly known in the Roman world as Verulamium. This place was fairly unbelievable. To think about seeing these things that have been there for over eighteen hundred years; these things were already a thousand years old during the Middle Ages. That is totally ridiculous. I actually vomited today after thinking about it. We ate lunch at a pub called the Ol' Fighting Cocks. Burgers were a mere seven and half pounds. For you Americans, that translates to FIFTEEN DOLLARS! Does that seem obscene to anyone else? Needless to say, I got a chicken sandwich with crisps. (A little translation help for you – crisps = chips, chips or fat chips = French fries. I had no idea until today, either.) On a side note, I really do enjoy the staff of the program here. They are really fun people. One dude is Australian, a couple Americans, and of course a few locals. All lovely people with a story to tell, they are. And I enjoy listening. As for the kids, there are definitely a few that I fancy more than others. Too many of these kids have spent their first week giving each other their resumes, as though they were out to prove how sweet they are. (Of course, I would never do such a thing.) Anyways, back to the church. This cathedral is pretty amazing, and it would definitely qualify as monstrous, which is something the pictures don't do justice to. It is named in honor of a man who housed a fleeing Christian missionary and was converted himself. Then he was mistaken for the man he was hiding and was executed on the spot where the absolutely massive Cathedral now rests. Historians actually don't even know for sure if this dude really was executed or if he even existed, since his most recent historian lived almost a thousand years after him in the 13th century. But it makes a cool story, regardless. This evening was spent hanging out a pub again – the Eagle and Child tonight, since we were at the Lamb and Flag last night. That pub scene would definitely qualify as baller. I saw the bartender snicker when I asked for a lime in my small Coke. So I punched him in the gut and fed his children to some mangy dogs roaming the alley down the block.

September 10, 2005; Saturday

One of the most famous characters in the history of literature, Sir Arthur Conan Doyle's Sherlock Holmes, remembered the great city in this way: "The air of London [was] the sweeter for my presence." I echo his same sentiments. There is no doubt in my mind that I left London in greater shape than I found it at roughly quarter to noon this morning. After our one and a half hour bus ride, we trekked into Trafalgar Square, which is quite fantastic. It sits in front of the National Gallery and just around the corner is the National Portrait Gallery. I tell you, these places were incredible. First, they are absolutely stocked with art. The size of the collections borders on ridiculous. As I tooled around alone, I found myself daydreaming that I was Thomas Crown, masterfully hatching an incredible plan to outwit the security devices and ably make away with Giovanni's fifteenth century *Agony of Christ* masterpiece. What a sweet story that would be to tell the grandkids one day. Alas, I walked out empty-handed; however, I was legitimately disappointed that my time was cut short just so that I could meet up with the rest of the group. The portrait gallery was also quite fascinating. Who knew how interesting it would be to look at people's faces intently and intensely? Every face tells a story, they say. I would alter that famous line a little bit: Every face may tell a story, but a lot of them tell a frickin' ugly one. Of course, I am kidding. Faces are beautiful. You are beautiful and so am I. And so is everyone else. No one is ugly and everyone is pretty. Ya know, I write those words and I giggle to myself because I have to admit that some of mugs I've seen in my day could put a dog to shame. Anyways, after the rains came during our sack lunch munch time, we decided to take a Tube trip to our next stop, which was called The Monument, put up to remember the Great London Fire of 1666. This fire was no joke, as it burned eighty percent of the city. But get this – six people died. Does that sound factually impossible to anyone else? Anyways, I decided to pay the two pound fee to climb to the top of this pillar-like structure, expecting neither the excruciating flight of stairs that took me to the top nor the incredible view of the city I had from up there. It was probably my favorite part of the day. From there, we walked to the Tower of London, where I spit on the left shoe of one of the guardsmen there and told him to go eat some more beef. (If that joke made no sense to you, type "beefeater" into a Google image search and see why I just made a hilarious funny. Man, I am a total riot.) We attended an Evensong at St. Paul's Cathedral in the evening (ironically enough). I tell you, beautiful voices can soothe the soul of even the most tired of warriors. (Yes, I just called myself a warrior. Walking London is no joke, you arm-chair tourists out there.) Here is a side note, talking with our group leaders was hilarious. This one dude, Simon, is hysterical. By the way, could there be a more fitting British name than Simon? And that is too bad, actually, because our Simon is Australian. Still a cool accent, though. Anyways, I apologize for this taking so long. Simon is uproarious. He offered to take a picture of me with my Elph camera. He takes it delicately in his hands and says, "Man, you could almost swallow this with a glass of water." If you didn't think it was funny, think of his accent and speak it again to yourself (out loud, of course). If you still didn't think it was funny, then you are wrong. We ate our dinner in China Town, which provided me with some sustenance which could have more accurately been labeled as "more sour than sweet chicken." Following that, a walk through the streets of London (including Piccadilly Circus) took us back to our bus. Talking with my roommates tonight, Anthony says something to this effect: "Did you know we're not supposed to wear any striped ties unless we have an affiliation with a certain club that endorses your color combination?" Matthew replies succinctly, "I paid twenty-five bucks for my tie, and I'll wear it when I damn well please." Apparently, as our comfort level with each other grows, so does our use of expletives. And I am totally comfortable with that. To be honest, I'd been waiting a whole hell of a long time to start cussing again.

September 11, 2005; Sunday

Easily the most boring day in Oxford to date. I got up and attended a high Anglican service at St. Gile's Church all by my lonesome. And that was about it. I could bore you with the rest of the day's happenings, but I choose not to.

September 12, 2005; Monday

We had a stretch of class this morning. That included part of the afore-mentioned video series, tea (Of course, we had tea. These people cannot get enough of that action.), and two lectures. Neither of the lectures were of profound interest to the average American. But the topic of lectures reminds me of one of my favorite moments of the semester thus far. It occurred last week. An Oxford don had come to our group to give us a lecture on John Duns Scotus. This cat was probably the most stereotypical Oxford don that has ever existed. His clothes mismatched horribly and were quite oversized. He wore a bowtie. He was little. Just the perfect picture of what he looks like in everyone's mind. He gets up there to talk about the philosophy of John Duns Scotus, a thinker from the thirteenth century. He begins: "Now, I know that because your sheets say so, you are aware that I will be talking this morning about Duns Scotus. Now your first question is probably this- who the hell is that?" It was hysterical. Moving on to the day's events, I spent the whole afternoon in the Bodleian Library. That place is ridiculous. For a cou-ple reasons - first of all, it is sweeter than homegrown corn in late summer or early fall. Second of all, you can't borrow any books there. Everything is considered a reference book and cannot leave the library. Getting acclimated to their borrowing system is a day and half job in itself. But once you get it, you are straighter than a heterosexual. And not only am I a hetero (con-trary to what several people in my life suspected for a stretch of a few years), I now know how to rent books at the Bodleian. Another thing about that place – it contains one of the most baller rooms I've ever been in. It is a read-ing room called the Duke Humphrey's Room. It is filled with so many old books that can't be touched (because they will probably fall apart) and you can't take pictures in there (for no apparent reason). It is so amazing, though. Obviously, a few-worded buffoon like myself can give it none of the justice it deserves. It reminds me of when we were little, and Dad used to give Jeff and I no justice in our simple request to own a Nintendo system. "First, I want you to type up a formal document outlining the pros and cons of your desire to buy a Nintendo system. Then, your mother and I will analyze what you have to say and give you an answer." Subsequently, in his supreme and unchanging judicial wisdom, he would promptly deny our request. No justice, Dad. No justice. Post-library, I visited the grocery store and couldn't deny the temptation of the frozen American-style meal of chicken strips and fries. The fries made me think of eating shoelaces, and the strips were more like chewing breaded rubber. I'll resist the temptation next time.

September 13, 2005; Tuesday

Last night, my roommate (the impressively intelligent but usually carefully kind one) asks me a question: "Do you think you'll ever write a book?" I respond: "Maybe. If I did, it wouldn't be a history book or anything. I know that. Will you?" Anthony comes back with, "Yeah. But if I do, I am pretty sure it will be a more scholarly work, something that requires a lot of research. It wouldn't be some worthless memoirs or something." Unbeknownst to the pain he had inflicted upon my soul with his comment (since all I write is "worthless," self-oriented commentary), I cried myself to sleep silently. Have I told you about my recent decision? In my doing my utmost to avoid being the victim of xenophobia, I have decided that I am going to use a British accent with all of the locals. Whether it is the checkout lady at the grocery store or the librarian at the Bodleian or the homeless snake lady that lives in University Park, I am going to give them my pleasantries with a strong dose of Brit in 'em. Wait, I think I just decided this will be a life change. Think about it. It works here because I fit in with everyone else. It works in the States because everyone loves the British accent. It works in the whole of Europe because you are a foreigner but at least you're not an obnoxious American. Are there even any other continents that I have to worry about? I know I have the three majors accounted for – the United Kingdom, the States, and the rest of Europe. I think Antarctica counts as a continent, but I'm sure they too, like the rest of the globe, will appreciate my newly acquired habit. Time will tell, I guess. I am boring you with these semi-worthless (There's that word again! Anthony's thinking has now infiltrated its way into my subconscious) line of thought because my day was identical to yesterday (minus the meal of shoelaces and rubber): lectures, study, etc.

September 14, 2005; Wednesday

I decided to take up drinking and smoking in my further efforts to fit in with the local yokels. And since I never do anything half-heartedly, it is going get pretty heavy pretty quickly. I'm talking three to four brews a night and probably a pack or so a day for this, the first week of my grand experiment. I will likely incorporate promiscuous sex by the time October rolls around. And since I already have the rock 'n' roll thing going on (Pearl Jam forever, man!), the only thing left from this magical concoction of fleshly happiness is drugs. Lots of 'em. And I just recently met a dealer from Christ's Church and one from the Parish of St. Mary Magdalene, so I should be straight. I send this to you as a warning mostly, so you folks back home won't be totally shocked upon beholding me in what will become my worldly paradise of a life. In terms of other activities, I seem to get the impression that you guys are getting the impression (a double impression, if you will) that I don't actually do any work here. This thought was furthered by a comment from Dawn in a recent e-mail. (SOME members of the close-knit community I call Brad-followers actually e-mail me back! Let that be a lesson to ya.) She closed her deep, sensitive, and very personal email with this line: *"try doing some work at some point :)."* What troubled me about this line was not the emotion that likely stuck out to you as a flagrant violation of the trust that exists between any brother and sister (and for which, she definitely needs to be scolded, now that I think about it more critically), but the tone with which she made this remark. It seems that she thinks I do no work. Au contraire, dear sister. I go to class from 9.30 til 1.30. (Yes, there is a tea break, but I don't count it because of my abstaining from the product of the hour.) I then spend the hours of 2 PM until 7 PM in the library. This is not messing around, I assure you. Be not misled, O followers of mine. Trust that your leader works his buns off, and does so tirelessly.

September 15, 2005; Thursday

Twice in the last two days, I've avoided the stop-and-chat. For those of you unfamiliar with the life and times of Larry David (*the main character on a television series--*), you may find that term to be an enigma wrapped in a riddle disguised as a mystery. I shall now divulge what it is at its very core. I have been walking about the streets of Oxford, all by my lonesome, and seen other members of the Visiting Student program. They clearly are looking for me to stop and muck it up with them (the stop-and-chat, if you will). For whatever reason, I decide not to partake because at that time in my life, the potential for conversation with said individual doesn't appear to me to be what I would call kosher. Don't get me wrong. It's not as though I slap them in the face (or whatever the social equivalent of that is). I exchange the distant head nod, perhaps a shoulder shrug, and I'm even generous enough to throw a rather meaningless smile, and then I turn from their direction (along with any possibility of further contact), hoping to not hear them call my name (which I might ignore anyways) and carry on my way. Keep in mind that the effects of such a decision (that of not allowing for the stop-and-chat) have the potential to be catastrophic. The person could possibly feel enormously slighted and wronged and take their pain, hurt, and anguish out on you by bashing your good name to the likes of everyone you know (which is not a good situation when you are already a stranger in a foreign land). But it seemed to me to be a risk worth taking. Twice. Will I receive a just punishment for my actions? Time will tell, ladies and gents. Time will tell. In other news, I finished my first paper of the semester tonight. I actually found the topic quite fascinating. It is called "[William] Wallace and [Robert] Bruce: What They Were and What They Have Become." (If interested, email me and I'll send it to you for your perusal.) I think it's decent, but when it comes back to me blood red from all the corrective marks, I won't think it's as decent. But that won't be for a couple days at least.

September 16, 2005; Friday

Ah yes, you remember me mentioning that paper I finished last night. Well, I woke up this morning and literally, half of the people living in my house were still awake working on their papers. One of them was one of my roommates. This dude does not fit the mold of the procrastinator, either. I would have pictured him as being done on Wednesday. But here it was – 2 in the morning last night and he had one page done. And he was doing his laundry of all things! Get your priorities straight, young man. Half of the other house also was up all night. That is 30 out of 62 kids! I mean, this is the first week. Are these people insane? I was nearly speechless, and I pretended like I really was a mute when they asked me when I'd finished mine. Anyways, today we visited the city of Winchester on one of our patented Friday field trips. It was quite incredible. We had this behind the scenes tour of the Cathedral there, which has been around since the Norman Conquest in the 11th century. We got to go up in the rafters of the giant nave, and climb these stairwells that were so so tiny – as in both of my shoulders touched the walls around me. And the stairs were only a couple inches wide – no stilettos allowed. Anyways, we went on top of the Cathedral's tower to get a sweet view of the city, and into the bell room and the bell ringer's room. It was amazing. If you ever go to Winchester, get the Cathedral tour. We also had a tour of Winchester College, which is not a college at all but really a school for 13-18 year olds. The school was founded by William Wykeham, who also did the most significant renovations on the Cathedral. His goal for this school was to raise 70 of the top kids in the country to be the nation's leaders. It still has an incredible alumni list – earls, lords, Parliament leaders, etc. There are 70 kids allowed over any five year span; so that means about 13 kids every year make this school through an application and testing process. Get this – our junior dean, Jonathan (the Hugh Grant dude) was one of these cats. Basically, so far in his life, it would not be possible for him to have had a better education. Mad respect. The school itself is quite the site also. When built, and for the subsequent 500 years or so, the place was entirely self-sufficient. It had its own brewery, stables, kitchen, etc. Everything. And also, it is illegal (as in English law) to take pictures of the 70 "scholars." They are identified by wearing around these black robes. Now, there are 800 students total but still only 70 of them are live-in scholars. And they have sick game.

P.S. Of course, I snuck a picture. As though you had to ask.

September 17, 2005; Saturday

Once in a lifetime, the eyes of my fans turn here, to this tiny hamlet in western England known as Dorchester. (Please tell me someone caught the Groundhog Day allusion.) What a cute, quaint little town. (The rumor is true. Men do use the word "cute," albeit sparingly.) We walked through the common paths, which by law are open to the public (even if they go through people's land or barns or anything), up to the top of this giant hill called a clump. The twin clumps that we climbed were basically the location of all the hubbub that went on in medieval Dorchester. No remains really kept, though. Now, it is merely the most beautiful of countrysides. Truly breath-taking. (Please tell me someone caught the Seinfeld allusion.) We ate our packed lunches atop clump number one, then made our way over to clump two before our descent through a veritable blackberry bonanza. (And more importantly, I discovered two more members of the worldwide fan base of the incredible modern Disney classic *Newsies*.) We closed out the trip with a stroll through the town, visiting its medieval cathedral, a local craft fair (featuring marshmallow fudge that couldn't be resisted), and a cute little square that sold us tea, coffee, and hot cocoa (the latter being for the more sensible of palates). More than one person seemed to fancy my one-word description of the experience. So I shall use it here again: delightful. Just delightful.

September 18, 2005; Sunday

I will open with a comment that one of my roommates (the often unintentionally funny one) made today. "I was sitting in church and thinking, 'I can't wait to get back to America and go to a restaurant and get a whole lot of food for just a little bit of money.' What's more American than that?" I laughed. Because it sure as heckfire cannot be done in these parts. Here, you're paying 3 American dollars for a small Coke and you feel like you're getting a deal. The folks that live here have it rough, I tell you. A life of bad burgers, first of all. (That's the real travesty in this discussion. Man, the burgers really suck here.) And then to make it worse, you're paying 14 bucks (or 7 pounds) for the meal. A lot of times, the burgers don't even come with cheese! As though people still eat HAMburgers anywhere! And then if you are the drinking type, you go out to a bar and get a beer, right? 3 pounds, at least. That is 6 bills in the states, folks. 6 bills. That's half a CD! I remember, when I was young and foolhardy, I would think in that capacity. I'd ask myself, "Man, I really would like a milkshake right now, but is it worth a quarter of a CD?" Sometimes I still do it. I go to a movie and pay something ridiculous like $8.75 (after the student discount), and I wonder aloud whether or not it's worth it. Of course, it's not. I always huff real loud when the ticket salesman tells me the price, as though the worker actually had some influence on the corporate fat cats that have decided to charge me that ridiculous sum to see Terminator 3 on the Ultrascreen. And I still pay it! That's the real wonder of it all. What the heck am I thinking forking over that kind of cash for that garbage? It is situations like these when the words of a disgruntled Jerry Seinfeld cannot ring more true: "What are we doing with our lives?!?"

September 19, 2005; Monday

So there are opportunities to join these different clubs here. My buddy Nathan is joining a rowing club. My pal Owen is thinking of joining a windsurfing club. There are wine tasting clubs, chess clubs, clubs to learn Russian and Portuguese. The clubs here are diverse and multi-faceted. What will I decide to engage myself in? Probably nothing. Why? Because I am scared. I am scared of the demands of my academic schedule. I am more scared of this semester than Dawn was of the Iceman in *The Commish*, starring Michael Chiklis. I'm not one to get scared, either. (I mean *The Ring* was good and all, but I definitely had clean undies at the end of it.) That's actually another thing that scares me – the fact that I'm scared. It's basically just a meaningless and plausibly endless cycle of fear and scariness. What to do, what to do... My paper this week is on Samuel Pepys. Have any of you boys and girls ever hear of Samuel Pepys? (By the way, its pronounced Peeps, as in the squishy sugarized gelatin bunnies that are sold around Easter at Walgreen's locations in your surrounding area.) Neither had I, before two weeks ago. It seems the dude kept a diary for a ten-year stretch between 1660 and 1669. This diary is considered a literary masterpiece, for a few reasons. First of all, it is basically the first diary we have for a stretch of time like that. Second of all, Pepys lived through some pretty incredible stuff: the Great London Fire of 1666, an episode of the Plague, several Anglo-Dutch Wars, not to mention some other meaningful action. Third, Pepys was incredibly open in his diary, as it is clear that he never intended anyone else to read it. He talks openly about his extramarital affairs, as well as his personal judgments on friends and colleagues and other very revealing things. My paper is basically about one aspect of his point of view, specifically his views on the Second of the English Wars with the Dutch, and more specifically what he contributed to modern history's understanding of the Dutch's attack on the English through the River Medway in 1667, which has been called the most humiliating experience ever suffered by the Royal Navy. So we'll see how that goes. Today on a short field trip, we visited the Pitt-Rivers Museum here in Oxford. This place is ridiculous. The guy who started it made this ridiculous ultimatum in order to get his collection on display: he made Oxford promise to always feature the junk he wanted or else all of it would be transported to Cambridge. (Cambridge, I was told by the Director of our program, is "that polytechnic school north of London". I sense a little bit of a rivalry.) Anyways, this museum is filled from floor to ceiling. There is so much stuff in it. The display cases are so close to each other and stacked atop each other. (At one point I had to squeeze my shoulders in to sneak in between a couple displays.) The artifacts there are featured typologically, as opposed to a normal museum that features items either chronologically or geographically. So all the hand-weaved baskets would be featured in one case, whether from Malaysia or the Alaskan Eskimos. All the religious masks, whether from southern Zimbabwe or the Peruvian summits, would be featured together. It is definitely an interesting scene, but there is a reason behind it. Pitt-Rivers was a social evolutionist, and he thought the best way to demonstrate the evolution behind people groups was to display his stuff with the least civilized (the Native American and central African tribes, according to him) next to the most civilized (the English, naturally), in order to see the differences. Interesting, huh?

September 20, 2005; Tuesday

A couple weeks ago I chastised you for not knowing who John Wycliffe was. I told you to question your salvation. A new development has arisen. Definitely, still vehemently question your heavenly citizenship (if you need to), but not for the reason of not knowing that Wycliffe was a martyr. Why's that? He was no martyr. He died a natural death. But he was still pretty hated; don't get me wrong. Actually, some years after his death, some jokers thought it necessary to dig up his bones and burn them to ashes. Messed up, huh? And get this - that was in 1993. No, just kidding about that last part. But that would have been a pretty crazy scandal, huh? Anyways, as long as we're on history again, I want to recount a story from when we were at St. Paul's Cathedral in London. It turns out that Queen Victoria had her 50th Jubilee of her queenship there in 1887. After it was over, she complained about how the joint was "too plain." This is one of the most fantastic cathedrals in the entire world and it was too plain, she says. So what did they do when it was realized that her 60th Jubilee celebration would be there, too? In the far section of the nave, they put these giant, beautiful and elaborate religious paintings up; they are gold and shiny and brilliant and cover the whole ceiling of the nave. Very striking. The queen would have loved them. Would have loved them? "But Professor Larson, why didn't she appreciate them if she had her 60th party there?" Well kids, her party took place on a hot day, and she felt too tired to climb the stairs that day. So they had her party outdoors to satisfy her. What a harridan. (For those of you wondering what a harridan is, all I did was type the B word into thesaurus.com and harridan came up. So you heard it here first. Queen Victoria = harridan.)

September 21, 2005; Wednesday

Well hello. I don't really understand the social interaction of people here. Right now, I think very little of the British pleasantries. There is a reason for that: they do not exist. No casual hellos, no friendly nods, no excuse me's. None of that goes on here. I know what you're thinking. "Brad, look who's talking. Twice in the last week or so you denied the stop and chat and also you are clearly not into the social scene." But folks, this really has nothing to do with my place in the social strata, nor with my (non)welcoming attitude toward the conversation of acquaintances. This is society. You say hello to people you pass on the street. You apologize when bumping into a person. You nod to the people you pass by. At the very least, you make some blasted eye contact. Here, you get Nothing.

(Notice the capital N.) I must be honest. Yesterday, I passed a policeman in the park on a bike. He made eye contact, gave the nod, and even moved his lips as though he had maybe thought about an actual greeting. I was taken aback. Astounded. Flabbergasted. The best I could muster was a "Hul…." and a severe turn of my head, which served no purpose since he had already sailed past me. Either way, the norms in this country are in serious disrepair. I can't wait to get back to the city sidewalks. The mall. The waiting areas at restaurants. There, people treat each other like humans. They converse with words. Such a concept is foreign in this place.

September 22, 2005; Thursday

I rarely think of Taylor. Strange, huh? I can't really figure out why that is the case. I know that those dudes are having tons o' fun without me, and yet, I remain unfazed. Weird, huh? Why would that be? Am I just too disconnected to realize what I'm missing? It's not that I am having such an amazingly fun time here. Don't get me wrong. I am loving being here, but I would refrain from saying that I am having loads and loads of limitless fun. I like the guys I live with, but I don't love them like I love the boys. It's different. Good different for sure. No complaints. I just can't figure out why I don't miss it more. But why dwell on that action? Today, we obviously watched the Schama video from 9:30 to 10:30, then a couple lectures, and then no lunch for the first time in these past few weeks. I enjoyed my plastic bag lunch in the University Park reading A Return to Modesty, which I am thoroughly enjoying. I realized today that the book is clearly written for women. She constantly asks direct questions to the women readers, and never refers to reading from a male perspective, which is fine. Anyways, I saw a sneak preview of the new Guy Ritchie movie – Revolver – with Nathan today. It defined cool, specifically Andre 3000's character. The movie as a whole is messed up and not explained at all. But very, very cool. And tomorrow: Bath.

September 23, 2005; Friday

Yes again, there were a ton of students that stayed up the entire night. Who are these people?!? Anyways, we took another field trip – to Bath this time. It was quite enjoyable. We toured the ancient Roman baths, where everyone who visits is subjected to listening to an audio tour with a personal headset that looks like an early 90's car phone except twice as long and it hangs around your neck. Personally, I think it is a ploy by the British government to make all of us tourists look like total morons. I would stand around some of these artifacts and look at all of us donkeys listening to these ridiculous summaries of the ancient Roman god's temple. It was actually quite embarrassing. I almost shot most of the people I was there with, but then I realized that if I was going to go that far, I should probably be willing to shoot myself. And I know that I got a lot of life ahead of me. So I held back… just this once. Cool place, though. Hit a pub tonight. We went to the Turf Tavern, which probably has one of the coolest locations in Oxford. You have to go down a couple alleys to find yourself there. You feel like a really really neat-o-keen secret agent when doing it. Tomorrow, I shall explore Hampton Court.

September 24, 2005; Saturday

A lonely day, some might say. Exploring the largest city in the most historically fascinating (my opinion, of course) continent in the world all by one's lonesome. Lonely? How could you call such a day such a thing? Liberating? Yes. Limitless opportunity? Yes. Lonely? Pardon my French, but heck no. I caught the Oxford shuttle bus into London and got dropped off at Victoria Station. After taking a good bit to get my bearings straight, I was fine. I took off down Victoria Street toward the Westminster Bridge, passing Westminster Cathedral, Westminster Abbey, Big Ben, and the Houses of Parliament in the process (sorry about all the Westminsters), crossed the bridge and made my way over to Waterloo train station (i.e. not the Tube.) Bought a ticket for Hampton Court, and found out that my ticket was neither collected nor even asked for. I have no real idea why anyone would ever buy a ticket at all. My only guess is that the punishment for not having a ticket when you are asked (if that ever happens) must be quite steep. Otherwise, no one would ever buy them. Anyways, it was about a 30-45 minute trip and then a 2-minute walk to Hampton Court. The palace was quite fascinating and the gardens were definitely somethin' else. I got an audio guide tour with my entry ticket to the joint, so I took four different audio tours – the kitchen tour, the William III tour, the Georgian rooms tour, and King (Henry VIII) and Queen staterooms tour. I was all toured out. Of course, before leaving I had to complete the maze in the gardens, which was equipped with state of the art hidden speakers featuring the random giggling and whispering of British children to taunt those who aren't frustrated enough with the entire concept. I made my way back to London (not needing a ticket, again, of course) and tooled around London for a good bit by myself. It was highly enjoyable as an experience. My one regret: I should have bought an Oxford Tube bus ticket instead of an Oxford Bus Company ticket. I wasted at least 45 minutes for the wrong bus. So I had that going for me, which was nice.

September 25, 2005; Sunday

Yet another boring Sunday. I am growing quite accustomed to these more laid back days of rest. How come no one pays attention to the 4th commandment anymore? We just dismiss it, as though God was just kidding. It seems like a bunch of bull to me.

Now, I will enlighten you with some of the more British things I have learned lately, speaking-wise that is. Today, our teacher used the term "as soon as poss" and everyone laughed. They also love the word "brilliant." I heard a tour guide use the word "whilst," which made my afternoon. They say fancy a ton, too. "Would you fancy a carrot?... Yes, he's my boyfriend; I fancy him quite a bit." The word "bits" is used ridiculously, too. "In the beginning of the lecture is going to be some dull bits. But then the more interesting bits will come at the end." "Cheers" is huge, too. And it can apply to a lot of different circumstances. Saying your farewells, or if a stranger does you a favor, or many other instances that I probably haven't yet encountered. Another thing I've noticed is how stupid we Americans sound trying to implement their lingo. I've heard an American (who's actually lived here for several years) use the phrase, "He's a fine chap!" I almost punched him. It sounded ludicrous. This applies in almost all situations, which is why it's a good thing that I implemented my British accent. I should be set.

September 26, 2005; Monday

Well, I got my first bombed paper back today. It contained such thrilling comments as "Evidence?" and "Explain what these are." But my favorite was the final comment: "Your decision to use out of date, poorly edited selections... instead of the excellent ones on the reading list badly affected the quality of your writing. Why did you do it?" A man, or a boy which the grading made me feel like, is humbled upon reading such words. Ah well, I have decided not to lose sleep over my failures, which apparently were flagrant and multitudinous. I haven't bombed a paper since the late 80s, so while I am shaken, I will definitely rise again to conquer, or at the very least, to reach new levels of mediocrity.

September 27, 2005; Tuesday

You wanna hear something I find fascinating? Guess what percentage of people in the United Kingdom attend a religious service of some kind on a regular basis. To give you a point of reference, about 40% of Americans claim to attend regular public worship, but it is estimated that that number is probably closer to 25%. Regardless, that number here is an astonishing 6%. 6 bloody percent. Does that shock you? Keep in mind, there is an established church in this nation. (I'm sure that relates somehow.) Even more shockingly, in a 2001 survey, 70% of Britons claimed "Christian" as their religion (and they were given the option of checking "None", if you were wondering), yet still, the majority do not attend a worship service of any kind. Just a little tidbit of trivial knowledge for you (which most of you probably think is worthless). Today we visited the Natural History Museum here in Oxford. Attached, you will discover a picture of me and the terrifying cheetah who guards the museum doors like Lurch used to guard the Addams Family estate. Another highlight of today: I took advantage of Burger King's 99 pence bacon double cheeseburger September special. A little piece of the US right here on Cornmarket Street.

September 28, 2005; Wednesday

When I told my mom on the day of my departure from the States that I thought it would be appropriate for my last meal in the States to be pancakes, I had imagined the reason for their appropriateness was that

124

I wouldn't be enjoying anything like them for the next three and a half months. Little did I realize... Tonight, the parents of a fellow student in my house visited her, the night before our fall break vacation begins. With them, they brought the makings for the most delightful of special treats: mother-made chocolate chip pancakes in abundance, since she was serving a house of twenty-four. I cannot express in words my joy upon their hitting my tongue. The explosion my palette and subsequently my tummy experienced was comparable to a 9.7 on the Richter scale of gastronomical enjoyments. Behold, the power of the thin, battered cake. Tonight made my life. And now, to compound my enjoyment during this spine-tingling period of my life: tomorrow, the adventure that the locals call Roma shall commence.

This outlines the itinerary of Brad on a five day holiday to Europe.

September 29 – October 4, 2005

Thursday the 29th: Imperial War Museum field trip, flight to Rome

Friday the 30th: Vatican Museum, St. Peter's Basilica, see the Pope's grave, go to the top of the St. Pete's dome, Spanish steps, out to dinner with the Cali boys

Saturday the 1st: Capitoline Museum (1st public museum ever), the Roman ruins, Coliseum, Tomb of the Unknown Soldier, Castel Sant' Angelo, dinner with Nathaniel

Sunday the 2nd: Roman Catacombs, Trevi Fountain, St. Ignatius Cathedral

Monday the 3rd: Maritime (Peter's) Prison, the Roman ruins again, rainy as   heck, read in St. Peter's square

Tuesday: Fly home.

Wednesday, October 12, 2005

Since we have last communicated, I have been to Rome and back. I have written papers and met tutors and performed all of the rigorous hullabaloo. But now... let me move on to the most important news of the hour. Of the year, perhaps. Few parts of a person stand out so much that it is consistently the first thing bystanders notice about he who stands before them. This thing taunts them, almost forcing them to think to themselves, "This person has style. This person has pizzazz. This person has… a moustache." That's right, ladies and gentlemen; I am bringing it back. All the way back. Most of you who saw pictures saw that I had a good thing going this past Janu-hairy. Imagine what that beast can become when given a month or two more. The stash has begun, folks. In conjunction with the Beard-off my roommate is celebrating with his friend across the seas, I was inspired to participate in a facial hair-off of my own, against myself, by myself, for myself. But this venture is not entirely selfish. This action is for all of you, as well… my fans. You will notice, after looking at the attached photo, that this glorious moustache is accompanied by a minute growth on the lower lip. Stealing the name from the "Create your own player" option of NBA Live 2003, I call this adornment my "flavor saver" (or, as it is more affectionately known in the streets… the flava sava). This saver of flavors, which allows me to enjoy the zest, tang, and zip of tastes hours after consumption, was not an idea of my own, but that of my afore-mentioned roommate – the master Matthew Gillikin of Covenant College. While many of you may never behold me in my moustache-laden flesh (who knows how long it shall grace me?), I invite you to embark on this journey of a lifetime alongside me, thanks to the device that technology has christened the digicam. All aboard, friends.

Sunday, October 16, 2005

I have decided upon a name: The Stash Dialogues. I considered The Chronicles of the Stash, but I decided against it for this reason: the name is hopelessly similar to that horrid and pitiful excuse for a film starring Vin Duh-sel, titled "The Chronicles of Riddick". I am embarrassed that I know that fact, and please don't hold it against me in future communications. Regardless, I thought the Stash Dialogues was much more appropriate because that is really what this whole experiment is all about: the stash and its interaction with the lucky few who encounter me while it carelessly rests above my grill. Now I know this will be hard for most of you to comprehend, but I was actually asked today whether or not I was growing a moustache. Is the man clueless? I have been sporting this bad mamma-jamma for nearly three weeks, man! "Of course, I'm growing a moustache,"

I yelled at this no-name joker, lacing that seemingly innocuous sentence with an appropriate amount of curse words and personal attacks on this gent's heritage and his family's social standing. Then I punched him mercilessly in the gut while reciting the 86th Psalm. He apologized and I kindly told him to shove off. He did. Another person I live with, we'll call her Myrna, told me that she found my moustache humorous not because of the entity itself, but because "I like it when people don't take themselves too seriously." She spoke these words casually, as though I were totally devoid of feeling and consciousness. As though my growing this moustache were not the most serious task I have ever undertaken as an individual. Her immature words speak to the moral decline of young America's attitude toward matters of the heart. I'm going to speak to Customs about having her and her kind removed from the States entirely. In the meantime, keep my stash and its growth in your hopes and prayers. It will need that much, at least, in the face of the senseless lambasting and merciless taunts.

The itinerary when Brad hosted his Mom, Dad, sister, Dawn, and Julie Shiltz, the young woman Brad dated for eight months. We brought her along with us as a "surprise" to Brad.

Thursday – Monday, October 20-24, 2005

Thursday – Surprise of semester/year! Julie is here!, walk around Oxford, train back to London, dinner at Zizzi

Friday – Madame Tassaud's Wax Museum, Burberry, Harrod's, The Lion King

Saturday – Covent Garden shopping, more shopping, Woman in White, late dinner at Zizzi

Sunday – the London Eye, shopping, birthday bash, Zuma (with Gwyneth Paltrow and Chris what's-his-face)

Monday – goodbyes, train ride home takes roughly 4 hours

Thursday, October 27, 2005

This week, I have been writing a paper on the relationship between Tom Paine's Common Sense and the Declaration of Independence. I pretty much finished up this morning. I have typically spent about 2 full days on my primary tutorial papers so far. That is much less than it is supposed to take you. Perhaps I am not doing a very good job, but I think the stuff I'm writing is pretty dang good. So take that. I finished it up this morning, and then attended this duh lecture on Machiavelli in the Historiography series. I have discovered this semester that I have a burning hatred for Historiography as a genre. It is more than just boring. It is tedious, and in my mind, worthless. The study of history in general as an art or science is of no interest to me. Keep in mind, I am just one man, and my opinions are not to be trusted as gospel truth. Anyways, regarding lectures in general, I get nothing out of any of them. I have resorted to bringing a book and hiding behind a person who possesses a larger frame. That way, I can read for almost an uninterrupted hour everyday. I say uninterrupted because I do occasionally pay respects with a head glance at the lecturer, who is oblivious to my disinterest. The amazing thing about it all is the attendance at lectures. There is no role taken. No one cares if you skip, yet somehow they are all well-attended. Personally, I go because I have a feeling that I will have to sign a document attesting to my presence at the end of term, but that is beside the point.

Friday, October 28, 2005

Today, I just wanted to get out, man. You know that feeling? When you've had too much Tom Paine and too much <u>Screwtape</u> and too much James Madison, and you just want to catch a ride in a convertible with its top down headed for nowhere with nobody but Van Morrison to keep you company. Yeah, that's what I felt like. Of course, I probably would have crashed in the first few miles, once I came to one of those tricky turnabouts or I would have been driving on the right, and therefore wrong, side of the road. But those first few miles would have felt like a tiny slice of heaven. Anyways, I missed school today. I wanted to watch movie trailers with Botso and Raul. I wanted to talk hoops with Downey. I wanted to get real with Granto 56. I just plain missed the boys today. I comforted myself reading the NBA Preview on ESPN.com, and that was actually quite comforting. But in the words of that Elton John tune, "Ain't nothing like the real thing, baby". Mama said there'd be days like this. There'd be days like this, my mama said. Tonight was the

Tolkien Society's Gandalf night, so there was fireworks galore. Or at least firework noises, since we were out of visual range.

Sunday, October 30, 2005

I watched X-Men 2 last night. It was actually quite sweet. Wolverine's character is the man. Hugh Jackman is an impressive specimen in the feature.

Wednesday, November 2, 2005

Time does really fly. You don't even need to be having that much fun for it to do so. You can be writing papers and not doing very much socially, and it will still fly by ya. That is what I have been doing lately, and it has been good for me. I don't really know why, but that is the kind of thing you are supposed to say when you are going through something like this, I think. I went to a pub tonight, with Tim (who I really like and respect), Anthony (ditto), Nathaniel (he's kind of a cartoon), and Luke (who is hard to take seriously). We talked about the global warming lecture from tonight's SCIO group meeting and then about politics. I laid it out for them: politics is a bunch of hullabaloo.

Thursday, November 3, 2005

I had my C.S. Lewis tutorial today. It was a thrill a minute it was. I get pretty nervous for those sessions, to be honest. I guess it is partly being intimidated by Dr. Plaskitt (who tells me to call her Emma but I disobey) and partly my lack of familiarity with English papers. Regardless, I think today's went fine. We discussed the finer points of The Screwtape Letters, which proved to be a very worthwhile discussion. I left feeling good about myself, which may or may not have been a misplaced feeling. Overall, I give today a decent rating.

Friday, November 4, 2005

Happy birthday to me. Twenty-two years, man. What in the world am I doing with my life? It was a good birthday, I think. To my surprise, I was wished a happy birthday twice within the first half hour of the morning. My plan of telling no one had been foiled by both the sheet that boasts everyone's special days and also by Julie, who informed Peter Dull via email that it was my 22nd. That little rascal. I studied most of the day. Got back around 6.30. Peter had made an apple crisp in honor of yours truly, much to the delight of myself and the rest of the house who also basked in the dish's deliciousness. Many thanks to Peter for his thoughtfulness. A good day, I would say.

Just before going to bed tonight, I opened up a letter I had actually received a few days ago from a one Mark Joseph Ahern. I delayed its opening figuring correctly that it was intended for my birthday. I have never received as thoughtful a note. Mark touched the innermost parts of me with his words. I cannot express my feelings as I read what he had written. Words don't exist for it.

Saturday, November 5, 2005

Guy Fawkes Day was celebrated tonight. That means more fireworks than any Fourth of July that I have ever lived through. It wasn't the quality of the works, but it was the sheer quantity that was set off in all different locations around the city, and apparently, the country. To add to the celebration of the 400th anniversary of the failure of Fawkes and his Roman Catholic buddies' Gunpowder Plot to assassinate the Protestant King James I, they burn Fawkes in effigy amidst an incredible 50 foot raging bonfire in the middle of the park for thousands to glory in. What a delightful tradition.

So, I bought theater tickets today. Yes, I can tell you are impressed. Quite the admirer of the arts, aren't I? Wait until you hear what I will be taking in on Tuesday night at 7.30 pm... You've heard of William Shakespeare? He's a hack. You've heard of the Globe Theater? It's a dump. You've heard of Macbeth, Hamlet, and Romeo? Sounds like a sorry cast to me. But have you heard of the 50-seat Burton Taylor Student Theater of Oxford? Have you heard of Maverick, Goose, Iceman, and Jester? Have you heard of the Naval Flying School? That's right ladies and gentlemen, approximately 48 hours from now, I will be basking in the glory of that masterpiece of the stage... Top Gun. Here is the official summary from the theater's webpage: "At the Top Gun Academy, America's finest fighter pilots hone their skills in the deadly art of aerial combat. Lt. Pete 'Maverick' Mitchell, a 'natural heroic son-of-a-bitch' is determined to prove himself the best of the best. Do you feel the need?" The need for speed, folks. I don't know about you, but I can't wait to see how the star of the show is going to portray that heroic s.o.b. attitude as well as Katie Holmes's man did a short 19 years ago, when Ms. Holmes was practicing the recorder in her mandatory music class right before her 2nd grade Science Fair. Yes, they plan on recreating an aircraft carrier and epic MiG fighter pilot battles on an oh-so-tiny stage. Sounds impossible, you say? Of ye of little faith. The real problem will be fitting that all-important sand court on the stage for the famous volleyball scene. Should be glorious...

Sunday, November 6, 2005

There are several areas in which I am strongly looking forward to getting back home. One is the food. Here, my diet is boring, unhealthy, and not very tasty. It'd be tough to live like this. Another is church. I am looking forward to sermons that last more than 11 minutes long. I'm looking forward to the worship at TU chapels. I am looking forward to going to church with someone I know. Yet another is Americans. Here, I find myself not doing things because I don't feel comfortable since this isn't my homeland. You know the feeling. Well, I might buy a baguette from that sandwich shop, if I wasn't a blasted foreigner. Or maybe you don't know that thought. I'm probably alone on that one. I am looking forward to watching ESPN, man. Boy, am I ever. It is tough here for that reason. I don't watch anything but the occasional movie. Television has its problems: no diggity, no doubt. But it has its glories, as well. And NBA 2Night is one of them. Of course the people: my family. I miss Jeff's jokes. I miss Becky's tolerance. I miss Dawn laughing at me. I miss Dad calling me "Dude." I miss Mom smiling quietly and watching everyone calmly. I miss my friends. I miss Julie making me laugh and her doing her thing. I miss Raul talking on the phone. I miss Botso not eating like a human. I miss Steedj laughing really hard. I miss Ahern, Boyers, and Lentscher wrestling (which I may never see again). I miss Grant talking about the ladies in his life. I miss Steebs being Steebs. I'll be ready when the time comes. I'll be ready.

Monday, November 7, 2005

I have started a new tradition with a few of the boys: a little thing I have called "Stat of the Day." Everyday of the season thus far, I have updated P-Diddy, Rossa, Moosie, and of course, Steedj-face with a tantalizingly fascinating stat regarding the NBA. One day it was the fact that a rookie on the Pacers is older than any of the team's starters. Another day it was that the Clippers are 3-0 for the first time in 20 years. I not only enjoy it, but they do, too. I hope. The NBA is so blasted sweet. How could I not love it so much?!? I wish I was the NBA. Not that I was *in* the NBA. I want to be the NBA. Of course it makes no sense to you! Did you really expect it to?!? Get a clue...

Crick 5 has got some serious camaraderie going on in my humble opinion. Clearly, we all like each other. We all play different roles and are very different people in very different stages of our lives with differing opinions on potentially divisive issues. But I got mad respect for the boys. These two got game like the Bucks, who, incidentally, are 3-0, one of only 4 remaining undefeated teams. Go Bucks.

Tuesday, November 8, 2005

Top Gun was worth every single p of the £4 student discounted rate I paid for it. It was indescribable, but I will not let that prevent me from making a sorry attempt at a report. The evening began as theater experiences often do: fifty students impatiently waiting in a crowded hallway for the Ron Howard-wannabe director (complete with bald head, red hair, and short stature) asking us to turn off our cell phones and also shamelessly promoting the refreshments. Or should I say refreshment, as in singular, since all they offered was extra tall cans of Jamaican Style Red Stripe beer, which naturally was allowed onto the stage. You'll notice I said onto the stage, and not into the seating area. I make this distinction because the two were one and the same. The stage was maybe ten feet by ten feet. The room itself was maybe thirty-five feet by thirty feet. Did I mention the fact that this showing was sold out? Surely, that doesn't surprise you, since a performance like this comes along once every couple decades apparently, as the original was released in '86. I convinced my fellow theaterite that sitting in the front row was the best choice, but that was not much of a decision since there were only three rows of seating, with the square stage being surrounded on three sides by the enraptured, and partly intoxicated, audience. The character introductions started everything off. Not long into it, we realized that Goose would be played by the lone African-Englishman, who incidentally played two other roles as well. But he by no means led the cast in the number of roles played. One of the two females played approximately seven roles, including Goose's wife (originally played by a then-uncelebrated Meg Ryan, believe it or not), Slider (yes, the male character Slider was executed masterfully by this stage beauty), and an elusive Russian fighter pilot (identified solely by the standard Soviet hammer and sickle emblem upon her Commie Red baseball cap). My proximity to the actors themselves was a semi-awkward experience. More than once, I had to pull my feet back so as to not trip the participants. Another time, Iceman, in the middle of an intense aerial battle, couldn't move past Cougar because my knee was protruding into the stage. (My bad, Iceman...) The show began somewhat uncomfortably, since Maverick was belting out "Highway to the Danger Zone" all by his lonesome while doing his best Eddie Van Halen impression on air guitar. Keep in mind he stood close enough for me to detect his halitosis. I thought that might be the most awkward point. I was wrong. That came about an hour later, during the love scene, when Kelly McGillis's character moved behind the audience and began crooning out "Take My Breath Away" while the audience gaped at the videotaped make-out session between herself and Mav. Another rough spot came during the forecasted volleyball scene, when three out of shape Englishmen thought that tearing their shirts off was essential to their re-creation of the fabled sand court battle. (Thankfully, the beefier, blacker Goose refrained from such an action, choosing instead to sport a cutoff Visa Rewards tee.) The dialogue throughout the performance was flawless. First of all, the script came directly from the movie. These actors obviously had selflessly devoted themselves to memorizing the very voice inflections and facial expressions of the timeless characters, much to the audience's enjoyment. Add to that the fact that everyone of them were Ray-Ban aviator sunglasses-wearing Brits doing their finest attempts at American accents throughout the show, and you have a recipe for delightfulness with a side of euphoria. I know what you're thinking... how did they recreate the battle scenes??? Good question. I'd like you to do something for me. First of all, stand up. Next, raise your arms so that you look like... well, an airplane. Now comes the fun part: make airplane noises implementing as much of your checks as possible. There you are... you are now a Navy MiG fighter plane. I know this summary has been long, but please realize that I have barely touched the depths of this performance's accomplishments. I predict sold-out shows for the rest of the week. I predict Tony Awards. I predict Hollywood contracts. Like Lt. Maverick's "heroic s.o.b. attitude," Top Gun's power knows no bounds.

Thursday, November 10, 2005

Socially, things have been improving. I have taken somewhat of a liking to staying in the kitchen for more than the mandatory fifteen to twenty minutes for the dinner meal. Of course, I keep busy in there still by putting away dishes or eating other people's food. I wouldn't say that I am there purely for social reasons, but I am certainly less apprehensive than I once was. The people in this house are very interesting personalities. I enjoy many of them; others appeal to me less significantly. But that turns out to be a good thing, since the countless differences between everyone lead to some truly great and meaningful arguments. I really enjoy listening to these people discuss topics from Steinbeck's literary approach in East of Eden to Locke's conception of property's value in a neo-capitalist society. The people here are so blasted smart. They are passionate about their beliefs regarding things I have never heard of before. I like a good argument, no doubt. In fact, people have complained that I like arguing too much. But I like to argue about why Kobe *must* have been guilty or why Keenan Ivory is the coolest Wayans brutha. Here though, I don't touch it. And it's not because I am afraid of getting blown away by the opposition. Well, okay, it is kind of for that reason. But more importantly, I have no idea what people are talking about! Wowza, these cats are smart.

Tuesday, November 12, 2005

Tonight it was Meredith's birthday, and Wes made this cake that I have named Choco-Bonanza. It was a little slice of cocoa heaven. I went to a pub tonight with a few of the boys: Drew, Tim, Luke, Nathaniel, and

Anthony. I like these cats. These kids have pretty incredible plans for their lives. They were discussing who in the program is most likely to be famous someday. I really have no idea who that would be, but I think Anthony is a decent guess, since in my view, it looks like he will be in the public sphere in some respect. And I think he will be good at what he does.

Thursday, November 24, 2005

I didn't realize until just now that it has been nearly two weeks since I've hollered at you. My bad on that. Well, here it is – Thanksgiving. The best day of the year for myself and my extended family. Does it get better than Turkey Day in Michigan? The answer, clearly is no. But I did have (probably) the best that Oxford can offer. We had a "Thanksgiving Dessert," put on by the host of magnificent cooks that reside here: Lauren, Wes, Meredith, Peter, etc. It was quite delicious. Crick 5 put on our hippest duds and strutted our stuff for the spectacle. It was quite enjoyable, if I do say so myself. One of the more humorous portions was listening to Tim recite how awful his day had been, which did in fact sound rather treacherous. This inspired my roommate Matthew to recount last Tuesday, which was "the worst day of [his] life probably." Of course, the night would not have been complete without Wes and Nathaniel arguing over the merits of public education or some related issue. I got to call the fam today, which both brightened and grayed my spirits. I exaggerate, because I am not all that down. Of course, I would love love love to be there but I recognize that it ain't in the cards, so I deal. It did sound like quite a delightful holiday though, and I am the only absentee for the occasion. To make it worse, Dawn tells me that the cuzes rented Willow, perhaps the greatest midget classic of them all. Pour salt on my only semi-painful wounds, why don't ya?

Saturday, November 26, 2005

Wow. Today was a good day. The real action started about 2 pm, also known as game time (who!). My roommate, Matthew, had helped to make it a true Thanksgiving bonanza by organizing a good ol' fashioned game of American football. Matthew contemplated several different strategies of dividing teams: east coast vs. west coast, former athletes vs. athletic embarrassments, English majors vs. everyone else. He finally settled on the traditional style of two girls picking teams. Guess who was second overall pick? That's right... yours truly. I announced Lauren's mistake of a pick to the world and got a few cheap laughs. The game begins. As quick as a hiccup, we are down fourteen nil. I assume the game is over, which was quite wrong. You see, their quarterback, Justin, apparently got the mistaken information that I was on his team, and he proceeded to throw three passes right to me. I, of course, caught everything that came my way, did my classic (and classy) T.O. impression (Do you know who T.O. is?), and was lauded as both a SCIO hero and a savior to starving children in Southeastern Europe. We ended up having to call it after the first overtime period yielded no scoring. In short, the game was incredible and a lovely time for us football-hungry Americans. (What am I saying... as though I have ever in my life been football hungry.) The meal began several hours later, and it was quite enjoyable, albeit featuring colder food than the mother-led feasts that I have been spoiled by these last twenty-one years. There was turkey and pumpkin pie and most of the essentials. The real fun began at about 9.30 pm, when National Lampoon's Christmas Vacation was popped in to the player. As my friend Drew said, "It's Randy Quaid's finest hour." What a uniting joy a Christmas movie can be. All is well with the world when Clark Griswold is alienating his neighbors and Cousin Eddie is kidnapping Clark's boss and Uncle Louie is scorching the Christmas tree. All is well, indeed.

Sunday, November 27, 2005

I had an amazing dream last night, and I remember a lot of it. I will share. You know Drew, who lives in the other 3-man room on my floor, with Peter Dull and Nathaniel. He is the intellectual whose genius is both astounding and foreboding. So him and me are boys in this dream, right? Yeah, we were totally boys. We got to this concert and it is a concert maybe of the Spice Girls or if it's not them, it is some group just like them. At the end of the show, I found out the story behind the concert. This apparently was the beginning of a reunion tour for this girls' group. And Drew just happened to be the love interest of one of the main ladies. During a press conference, Drew was up on stage with this lady of his and I heard their story from her mouth. These two had been together when the girl group was first together. They ended up breaking up. But then recently, Drew had called her and they had gotten back together, and in turn, so had the girls' group. That is related because I then found out that Drew had written all of their songs. I, of course, had no idea of his music-writing abilities and was wowed by his awe-inspiring humility, since he had never made mention of his skills. The whole time she was telling her story, she was staring right at him while he held her hand. He was sitting next to her Slater-style in a chair, staring at her. It was a beautiful scene, and I've thought about it several times today. I loved it because it was like those two were having this incredibly personal moment right there yet they were in this very public press conference, and I got to watch it all. It was a privilege for me. This whole thing relates to the esteem I hold Drew in, I think. I was witnessed both Drew's humility and the way he gave himself to his relationship. Both moved me. It was such an awesome dream.

Tuesday, November 29, 2005

Everyone is hating on me because I am basically done with the long essay. Some kids haven't started; some are annoyingly nervous; one is done. It is me. I am him. I am annoyed that people are annoyed with me for being almost done. I honestly believe that I could start the whole thing over today and still be fine. Maybe that is optimistic, or maybe my paper just isn't that good. I don't know. I guess we'll find out. All I have left until the end of term then is really the take home exam (1800 words), and I have the research done for that. Basically, I will read a lot, I am thinking. The time from now until the end of the semester is the same as when traveling Eastern Europe begins to when I get to the States. We'll see how fast it goes.

Wednesday, November 30, 2005

We were chatting today at dinner, and somebody commented on how they were going to miss somebody. I said something and then I was asked what I'm going to miss. I don't really know. I'll miss the boys: Crick 5, that is. I'll miss a few people: Drew-nuts, Peter Dull, Owen, Nathaniel Fischer (as though I will ever meet another like him). The buildings, I'll miss. Maybe I will miss stuff. That'll be a question to answer in a month, and then again in six months, and then again in 5 years.

Friday, December 2, 2005

Tonight was fun. I went to the Vines through a pouring rain. I had to be convinced to go there, since biking through the precipitation did not excite me. But I am glad I did. We played this fairly fun card game called Snap. Tim, of course, entertained me and the rest quite effectively. It was a good time. Maybe I have been missing out by not hanging out there all semester. It seems like a pretty fun joint. Alas, time is up, and the semester is over (basically).

Saturday, December 3, 2005

And so I am in to law school. At least one of them. Marquette University. I am one for one. I talked to Mom and Dad today, who, while I was on the tellie with them, opened up the magic envelope. I called them thinking that none of the three envelopes Mom had emailed me about were acceptance letters (two were from MU, one from SLU). As I was dialing, I imagined, "What is it going to feel like if this is really it? Will some great feeling come over me?" It didn't. It was just one of those things. She read it. I heard it. It was a nice feeling, but not overwhelming. It's safe to say I liked it, though. At least I'll be in somewhere, I guess. Perhaps adding to this was my opening up <u>Planet Law School</u> for the first time yesterday and being effectually intimidated. Whoa. I was kind of reeling after going through about sixty or so pages of it. Dang man. It said the first year is commonly looked back at as the worst year of a given graduate's life. The outlook is not bright. Julie went crazy when I told her. It was nice to have somebody do that for me, since it clearly ain't my style. She took care of that route, though. So I had that going for me, which is nice. She encouraged me to go out and get tanked. So I did. Well, to be more accurate, I went out with others and watched them get tanked. And I mean tanked. Tim got pretty sloshed. And I was a sober witness to it all. I did feel almost totally out of place. I hate answering questions about why I'm not drinking. It is just annoying, that's all. I enjoyed the evening, I would say.

Sunday, December 4, 2005

Oh man. I have been getting loads of comments these last few days about how open I have become. "Brad, you talk!" "Brad, what has happened to you lately?!?!" "Where has this Brad been all semester?" It is nice to hear, I suppose, but I don't honestly know the reason any of it is occurring. I have just been more willing to assert myself for some reason, much to the amusement of others, apparently. A lot of it has to do with my budding relationship with Tim, a.k.a. JCR President. I think he is hysterical, and he can get me going pretty good. That has helped me out. Also, I have just naturally been getting more comfortable with those in the house, perhaps because of the time passing. Perhaps because I have been a bore all semester and want to be remembered as a rabble-rousing, rambunctious type. Perhaps because I will never see any of these people ever again in 2 weeks, and I just don't give a damn! (Pardon my French, but it seemed appropriate here.) Either way, I had my first big argument of the semester today. And I know argument has a negative connotation, but one could just as easily call it a debate. I don't really even care about what I was discussing, but it was fun and got laughs from spectators. I started it all by myself. It was about why girls wear jewelry. Hopefully, it's not to attract men (cause it's failing); hopefully, it's not to attract women (cause that would be wrong, as it incites jealousy). What other reason is there? It was basically Matthew, Tim, and I versus Nicola, Kathy (Matt's woman), Rebecca, and other random girls. Highly enjoyable. Then tonight, we were watching The Jackal with Richard Gere and Bruce Willis. Another great adventure. A decent movie, until the end when it becomes terribly unrealistic and implausible. That got me and Matthew going versus Tim this time, since he wanted to defend the picture as a respectable piece of the American film canon. We took him to the laundry (which is ironic, since Matthew hasn't been there all semester).

Monday, December 5, 2005

It is definitely long essay season. Everyone's anger toward me regarding my efforts has mostly subsided, I would say. It is all people talk about, though. I am amazed at the procrastination found here, a much higher percentage than that found at TU. The best instance was this one. About

5 o'clock, I walked into Tim's room, asking him if he wanted to partake of a film this evening. "Sure, what time?" he responded. We settled on 8.30. Then I got more into the situation. He has 44 of 379 pages read so far. Those are pages he needs to read before he *begins* writing. As in he is maybe 15% done with his research. And he had thoughtlessly agreed to watch a movie tonight! The man is insane, yet a genius who will graduate summa cum laude from a very difficult honors program at Biola University.

Tuesday, December 6, 2005

The long essays have been handed in. Everyone managed to get one in, so all that worry for nothing! What do you know?!? I'm shocked. Tonight, we had a bit of a Christmas celebration at the Vines. It was quite lame at first, since we weren't doing anything. Then the fun came around when the white elephant game began. My autographed bandana was a big hit (although it was the second last gift picked), as was Matthew's wife beater (which, incidentally, has not been washed all semester, unless you count bathing it in the sink with dirty underwear and 82p "Soapflakes" washing). A rambunctious game of spoons then unfolded, culminating in a battle over a single utensil between Tim and myself. I was stuck with the slippery handle end, if you want to know how it turned out. It was a fun night, though. In fact, my latest night yet in Oxford, although that had nothing to do with the party. I was somehow cajoled into starting and finishing the Jack Black classic *School of Rock*.

Thursday, December 22, 2005

The day has finally come. And I do mean finally. I have been awaiting today with incredible anticipation for roughly a month. I think that is about right, since Thanksgiving was roughly the starting point for my insatiable desire for the familiar. And now, in roughly ten hours, it will be quenched. I will board the plane in approximately thirty minutes. Man, it will be glorious. These past couple weeks have been a veritable whirlwind. Of course, the semester ended without much hullabaloo. All the take home exams were turned in on the 8th, then on the 9th we had a meaningless meeting at the Vines, where we all reflected on what an enriching experience we've just enjoyed. Hugs were shared by most, few by me. I will miss a couple of these cats: no doubt Anthony and Matthew, since I couldn't have asked for a better rooming situation; Tim, since he just strikes me as an entertaining personality; Meredith, who just helped to make everything more fun all the time; Jonathan, because he is entirely and wholly likable, despite the lack of any real conversation I ever shared with him; Dr. Baigent, because with her absence from my life comes the exit of the most accomplished human ever to grace this earth; and Drew, because never before had I met a true 21-year old intellectual, and because every word he spoke I respected with the authority due a sacred scribe. That might be it.

These last 12 days, I have done more traveling than you can shake the proverbial stick at (I know I'm not supposed to end a sentence with a preposition, but I remember the words of Winston Churchill in this age-old argument: "This is the sort of English up with I will not put."). Trains, planes, and automobiles. And busses. And rickshaws and hovercrafts. Okay, well not those last two, but they were added merely for emphasis. I've slept on all of those transportation devices as well. I developed an uncanny ability to sleep on trains specifically. It was as though nymphs would be playing their magical harps as soon as I put my noggin against the headrests, and I would be out. Nearly every time. Anyways, more importantly we visited cities that I may or may not ever see again: Budapest, Hungary; Vienna and Salzburg, Austria; Prague, the Czech Republic; and finally Krakow, Auschwitz, Warsaw, and Poznan, Poland. Wow; that is unbelievable. All in ten days, too. Granted, we surely did not do justice to any of the cities we saw in that short span, but I was happy to move on after each adventure, if only because it meant I was one step closer to that incredible moment of joyful reunion, not only with humans but with the American (and Christmassy) aura that, in a way, defines all born within its boundaries. Our visits in each city were basically the same, and they somehow all start with a C, much like the stereotypical youth pastor's message of salvation, whose points all magically correspond to the same opening letter. They were cathedrals, castles, and Christmas markets. The first two are understandable; that last one may be a mystery to you, as it was to me a short two weeks ago. These markets are literally littered around the ghettos of the Eastern half of Europe. They feature a countless array of decorated booths, selling such magical goodies as nutcracker chess pieces, tree ornaments featuring the local area's most notable attractions (which in at least three of the cities we visited was Wolfgang Amadeus Mozart), and also culinary delights like crepes, nuts, and delicious pastries. I may sound cynical, but I really did enjoy all these spots, if only because they reminded me of that feeling that I was so conscious of missing back in the blessed Midwestern US. I traveled this whole time with four other SCIO cats. There was supposed to be six of us total, but one dude was trying to save a couple bucks on the bus to the airport, and his frugality cost him, since he ended up not making the flight to Poland and therefore, access to the rest of the continent. Ouch. We all felt pretty terrible for him. It was unfortunate for another more selfish reason, as well. Luke was the one person I really knew before going, and the person I bought my tickets with, as well. I have no idea what he actually ended up doing, either. My guess is he chilled with Jonathan in Oxford, passing time at the Bod studying topics that interest him, since there are thousands of those for this kid. Traveling partner number one was Daniel Purisch. Daniel was essential because he had an incredible ability to read train times in foreign languages, despite knowing none of the languages.

Chapter 8

∞

MISCELLANEOUS DIARY ENTRIES

"I want my parents to think I was a good son, my siblings to know I love them and my friends to miss me."

BRAD LARSON,

response in an email exchange with a friend when asked how he
wanted to be remembered at his funeral

IN *this chapter, we have chosen to include a variety of diary entries, emails, and other items found on Brad's computer that reflect his humor and how he dealt with situations he faced as a student.*

4/28/01

....Went to the Brewers' game with _____, _____, and _____. We had to park at the VA hospital. We walked out the wrong entrance. Big mistake. We sat outside for 30 minutes before deciding to jump the fence into a construction zone so we wouldn't have to walk around the stadium. Oh, yeah—right next to 6 cops. We got caught. They frisked us and called in the sheriff and he told us if any of us have any history of trespassing, we all go down to county and have $300 bail. We all said "No". Then _____ remembered, "Oh yeah, I blew up a bus at 4 AM." For some reason he checked out negative. Praise the Lord. "Get outta here," said the cop (who was at half-mast). We laughed for a while. We were so lucky.

5/26/03

Just on a totally random side note, I've just been thinking the last few days about what a person (as yourself) might think of me if they read what I write in these notebooks regarding girls. I am sure they would think me deranged, obsessed, and unhealthy. They would see me like a variety of girls. I just wanted you to know that I consider myself pretty normal. The only difference is that I have written down my thoughts and now look back upon them and realize what an Idiot I was. I would venture to say that most guys have it pretty bad for one girl at all times. But all that will go for nothing because he will forget about it. Yes, when I read all this I feel like an idiot but I'm glad I wrote it down. So bear with me as you read all this useless jargon and remember that you too were probably an idiot when you think about the infatuations of your past. Am I right or am I right?

12/27/03

......_____signed on to Paradise Poker, won back his money and then quit. So he's dead even now. Then I told them my gambling thoughts that I got from this summer's financial Bible study. About being a good steward to God's money apparently, had some effect on him, 'cause he got back to dead even and then cashed out for good (at least he says). I think that's pretty exciting. And it's all because God gave me the guts to say something I didn't think would be well received. But, thank Him, it was!

12/30/03

...then I wrote a few thank you notes and for some reason I picked up all the cards I got from graduation. People said such nice things. What nice people I am blessed to know. The one from Tim and Sarah Aalsma almost made me cry. I had picked them up hoping to throw them away but now I hope I never do.

Brad was the Best Man at Jeff and Becky's wedding. These are the entries surrounding the weekend of the wedding. He gave a very humorous "Best Man" speech; it was a great hit!

6/17/04

Ah, the wedding festivities have begun. And I got to see them all unfold since the weather prevented any/all work from being done. Jay and Lynda arrived oh, say, 4:30PM. About 5:30PM, I get a call from Woody who says him and Julie were delayed and wouldn't be here until about 8.

He asks, "So what are you all doing?" "Oh, everybody is just sitting around and talking and stuff." And then he, in his oh so Woody, accent/tone/voice: Yeah, that cool. That's cool." Can't you just hear the guy saying it? Oh, the joys of knowing the one, the only Woody and Tati (*family friends from California*). All of Jeff's boyz arrived tonight, too. I'm not going to lie—there are one or two duhs in the mix this weekend. But being honest, I am cohorts with a duh or two myself.

6/18/04

Well, we got up early for JAGS-Jeff's Awesome Golf Scramble. Me, Pops, J, and Pelz were first off the tee. Through 9, we were one under. Then we traded Dad for Jeff's med school bud Jake and somehow finished one over. Oh well. We had a good time. This afternoon was o.k. The rehearsal itself was fine, although a bit long. We seemed to have arrived a little late, but we, the wedding party were unaffected. Said our hellos. Kathy and Chris and kids were in. Ken and Anne and Todd and Connie and kids. Both Grams. And I met my Uncle John and Aunt Margaret tonight. Yes, I met them. Dawn and I sat with them, actually sat with them, and Dad's parents and the Bellitos. It was pleasant. Jeff and Becky shared. All of it was touching. Jeff's to me tugged at the heartstrings. It was all good. Grandma would lean over to me every few minutes to tell me how long the people were talking, or that all this respect and marriage stuff sounds great, "but what if you marry a jackass?" That's a direct quote. It was long but very very good. Tomorrow is the big day.

◌◌

Brad's Best Man Speech:

When it was revealed to me a few weeks ago that it is customary for the best man to give a speech at the wedding, I did what any normal guy would do: I googled "best man speeches" on the internet. The sites were very helpful. First they said—tell some jokes. I found this one: A woman was telling her friend, "It is I who made my husband a millionaire." "And what was he before you married him," asked her friend. The woman replied, "A multi-millionaire." Next, the site said to mention some of Jeff's past exploits. Well, to be honest, in terms of girls, I never thought I would be more impressed with my big brother than when he was in 3rd grade, and in the middle of class, he ran up to his cute-as-a-button student teacher and gave her a kiss. No joke, he seriously did that. That was a tough accomplishment to pass up. But it seems that here today, as he sits next to his lovely bride, there is no doubt he has transcended that seemingly insurmountable obstacle. The next pointer I got off www.bestmanspeeches. com was to close with some sentimentality. Well, here it goes. To be honest, before Jeff left for college, our relationship needed some work. We bickered as all brothers do, which was understandable considering our differences. Jeff was musically inclined with that tap dancing and "song and dance" group and all; and I was more into athletics. Jeff never doubted his calling to be a doctor like our Dad; I'd always known I didn't want to be a doctor. Jeff excitedly attended Taylor; I reluctantly followed him there four years later. But it has been in my time at Taylor that I have been awakened to how much my brother has affected my life. Jeff has it all together. He has an unmatched work ethic, which is being severely tested right now in medical school. In light of today's events, he has a lovely and beautiful wife to look forward to coming home to every night. Finally, the two seem to have a future so certain that I feel like I could write their life story right now. Oh, what I would give for those things. So, I thought that this was a decent time to let them know how nice it is to be able to say, "I want to be just like my big brother when I grow up."

∞

6/19/04 (*Jeff and Becky's Wedding Day*)

Success. The day is over, and it was good. It ranks near the top of 'em, I tell ya. After a neck-shaving emergency visit, the real action started about 1 PM. Pictures didn't start until 2 and they took a good bit. That included "the interviews" in which no questions were asked and instead tell Jeff and Becky how you feel. Anyways, one of the funniest things all day was when the groomsmen were sitting in the church basement and Mark discovered a WWJD board game. This thing was seriously twisted. "Your little sister tells you she's attracted to girls. WWJD?" or "Your husband of 2 years slaps you in the heat of an argument. WWJD?" Some of the things/all of them, there is no set right/wrong answer. Anyways, the ceremony was lovely. Becky looked, of course, gorgeous and Jeff was his cool self. No tripping or any of that. After short hellos, the stretch Navigator trip began. It was a lovely party in there. Some of those jokers, man. Well, they are jokers. We drove downtown to the pavilion/park across from the art museum. After a quick battery change, we were off to the Women's Club for the reception. We made our entrance and my favorite part of the night took place: Dinner at the head table. It was so nice to just sit there and muck it up with the newlyweds and eat and stare at people and talk with Jeff about the people we stared at. No joke, I loved it. My speech took place after the meal but before the amazing raspberry dessert, sandwiched between Sara's and Rachel's speeches. Now, my delivery could have used some work, but the material was gold. Peeps loved it. My three biggest compliments: 1. Sue Davidson: "I hadn't cried all day until you, you little sh*t!" 2. Some unknown in the john who I urinated next to: "Great speech. One of the best I've heard." 3. Nick Crawley, who comes up to me and shakes my hand: "Great speech, man. You had me laughin' pretty hard back there." That means I appealed to all crowds. Then all of a sudden, all Jeff's friends warm up to me right after like a microwave. Apparently, they thought I was some quiet, shy, bad-speech-writing-loser. I showed them, huh? Then after the special dance numbers, peeps started to get their freak on. After, Aiden came up to me and dragged me on the dance floor. I figured it was time for me to drag every other cousin out there to make me look silly. It was a good night. And now, Jeff and Becky are engaging in intercourse.

∽

DURING *the Lighthouse India Mission trip in January 2005, Brad became good friends with Julie Schilt. One of the ways they interacted with each other was by the written word—asking and responding to questions in a spiral note-*

book. *The following are some interesting insights into Brad's preferences as re-corded in those exchanges.*

What makes you happy?

-Vanilla Cokes, but not the Coke-brand Vanilla Coke. It has to be like a fountain Coke with a squirt of real vanilla flavor

-Giving really good gifts that I thought of all on my own and then the person's genuine reaction

-tater tots with hot cheese

-not being able to fall asleep on Christmas Eve

-frozen "Reese's Peanut Butter Cups"

-impressing my brother

-listening to Norah Jones' first CD

-going to a Buck's game

-Philip Yancey

-finishing a book, even if it stinks (actually, more so if it stinks because I am not as happy if a good book ends)

-my Mom's pancakes loaded with butter but never with syrup

-Kraft Mac and Cheese spirals with little bits of hot dog chopped up in it

-emails from people I love

-movie previews

-finding someone who is obsessed with "Ground Hog Day" (but this only happened once)

-making people laugh

-people making me laugh

-cool Nestea after being really, really hot—but it has to come from a can

-a good game of Trivial Pursuit

-playing Jeopardy

-waking up without the aid of an alarm and not being tired. That is when I feel most rested

-Philippians 1:21-"*For to me, to live is Christ and to die is gain.*"

-family Thanksgivings

-travelling

-vacations
-returning after vacations
-Mr. Mark Daniel Van Ryn, my favorite person in the world. I love this
boy
-sunshine
-sunrises and sunsets
-the stars
-Roald Dahl books and short stories
-Christmas movies
-Christmas lights that aren't really tacky
-thinking about my brother's wedding
-being at my brother and sister-in-laws apartment

What are your favorite books? (most impactful)
Soul Survivor—Philip Yancey
What's So Amazing About Grace?—Philip Yancey
Mere Christianity—C.S. Lewis
Putting the Amazing Back Into Grace—?
Disappointment with God—Philip Yancey

Favorite movies? (movies I've seen the most times)
Groundhog Day
Hoosiers
Good Will Hunting
Shawshank Redemption
Legends of the Fall

Favorite CD's?
Van Morrison--Moondance
Bob Dylan—Blood on the Tracks
Paul Simon—Graceland
Pearl Jam—Ten
Collective Soul—Discipline Breakdown

Favorite Tom Hank movies?
Sleepless in Seattle
You've Got Mail
Castaway
Big
Green Mile

Describe what your life will be like in 10 years (in detail).

If God shines down on me and grants me the desire of my heart, I will have a helpmate. And she is <u>fantastic</u>. Only that word is not sufficient for her (a word that can describe a circus should not be applied to my wife). Perhaps glorious. Doubtless, she will have made a grave mistake in lowering herself to marry me but I will spend the rest of my life doing my darndest to make her forget that fact. I won't go to bed if I am not right with her. I will pray for her always. Most of all, I will love her. Oh yeah, she will be at my beck and call. She will submit to me unquestionably. Hopefully, the time it took you to turn the page of this notebook gave you enough time to smile and maybe bite your lip a little bit because that was kind of funny. So to be clear: these last two sentences were a joke but the previous stuff was not. Depending upon the mercies of the fertility gods, I will have approximately 1.75 kids. (I wore briefs until age 14, so keep me in your prayers.) They are really funny and love their cousins. My wife is really funny too, by the way.

I will teach my kids all sports, but I will love them more when they dedicate themselves to basketball (once again, just kidding). We will have family game nights because that's how much I love board games. I will be involved at a church that I love, where the pastor is a great speaker and he at least knows me by name if he's not a friend of mine. I will likely live in the Midwest (maybe Wisconsin, maybe not). I have a fascination for Colorado (my favorite state in the union because of its beauty, majesty, and ski hills). However, I would probably retire there or maybe move there later in life. I don't know if I will be there by 31. As for occupation, I would love to be a writer. I would love that because I like to write, and I think I could be good at it someday. Maybe I would work out of the house, maybe not. I will drive something fairly common like a Camry or a

Maxima. I will probably not have any facial hair but no guarantees. I will do my quiet time in the morning—outdoors, weather permitting. I like the idea of closing the day in prayer with my wife. That would be a good finish.

∞

DURING *his 2005 summer serving as a counselor at Upper Peninsula Bible Camp (UPBC), Brad developed a strep throat and was pretty much "cabin ridden" for 3 days. After this illness he wrote this in his diary:*

Blessings I have gotten through my strep:
   -seeing other's kindness and care for me
   -a break from counseling which I didn't think I needed, but apparently did
   -time to read/pray/write
   -chance to play cards with Sooz and Lisa
   -receiving everyone's prayers
   While at the UPBC, Brad had an opportunity to take time out and gain an appreciation of common things we often take for granted:

7/11/04

A camper named Ethan said something this week that caught my attention...a plane flew over our heads and a conversation continued with no pause. Then the aforementioned Ethan said "Here—a vessel carrying who knows how many people with who knows how many tons in it flies directly over us who knows how many feet, and we are so used to it that we don't even glance at it." Two good points, I thought. First of all, we humans are capable of some unbelievable things: we construct buildings over 100 stories tall, we harness the power of a river in a process I don't even understand, we send vessels to other planets, we take someone's heart out and give them a new one that works better. The new Milwaukee Art Museum—yeah, somebody actually thought of that design and said, "Let's try and build it." Or how about this: "let's build chairs that climb hills covered with snow and then give people a couple long pieces of plastic or metal or whatever to shoot them back down the hill and then let's charge them exorbitant prices and tell them its fun." And it has worked! I certainly bought it. How the human mind conceives of such things is inexplicable. The imagination is a gift and I need to use it. Second of all, we get bored too easily. We watch a giant object leave the atmosphere and we turn the channel. We watch footage of the President shaking hands with the President of Tajikistan and we wonder why they interrupted the Seinfeld rerun. We pass Miller Park as its roof opens up like a Honda Accord on a starry night and we don't even think of pulling over to behold the architectural display. A plane flies over our head and we don't think it's even worth a glance. How do we justify not caring about such things? How amazing are the things we do every day, yet it has become so routine that it is not worth noticing? Someone tells us our breath stinks, so we jack a brush in there with some blue stuff on it and push it around. If we have to write something down, we can all do it, but we do it with a style and penmanship that is unique to us, yet all who read it understand the meaning. We are a country of over 270 million peeps (approximately) and not one of them writes just like I do. (Now, there are a few exceptions to that rule, like David L. Larson, who only his secretary and immediate family can read.) Seriously, though, penmanship and its uniqueness is an incredible thing. We flip a switch and someplace dark now has light. We slap our arm when we feel something bite it and a creation of God dies. Does not even the mosquito have something to offer? We stick a Pop Tart in the toaster and are soon greeted with its aroma. Have you ever thought about that? Why do things smell good? We do things every day that should amaze us and they don't. Every day I get up and read words written thousands of years ago and from the Creator of the Universe, and I am seldom taken aback at that reality. Conclusion: we humans are so infatuated with our own little worlds and our own little problems that we miss the daily opportunities to let the glories of your basic day sink in. Abre los ojos. Open your eyes.

8/9/04

I cannot adequately describe to you my feelings at this moment. I am so blessed, beyond all belief…I had a so-so day at work and got home about 11PM and for whatever reason, I decided to check my email, despite having to get up at 6:30AM tomorrow. Oh, the joy and laughter the three e-mails I received brought me. From three of my favorite people—Laura Van Ryn, Andrea Butcher, and the unequatable Marc "Raul" Belcastro. I laugh like a child when I read Raul's e-mails. I wish I could read them forever. The written word is a powerful thing. All know that. But the written words of a friend can have a greater effect than almost anything. I will have a hard time going to sleep tonight thinking of Laura's thoughtfulness and humor, and Andrea's encouragement and Raul's indiscernible genius. Their writings are genius and I proudly say they are also my friends.

∞

Brad loved life and noted this fact frequently in his diary:

9/21/04

…here is a very random thought: I really enjoy life. Pretty much every stage I've thus entered I have liked better than the former. Now, if what Jeff says is true, then the next stage (post-college, not marriage) will be a bit of a letdown. I think I'll be able to deal with it. At least, I hope so. But for real, every day has it's own reasons to rise out of bed. I really just like being alive, experiencing things. It's a pretty sweet gig, this thing called life.

10/18/04

…today was a day when life was enjoyed. For some reason, at dinner I had this amazing and somewhat indescribable feeling that all is well with the world…

11/1/04

Ahhhh…the week! Normal people pray for the weekend and bless its arrival. For me, it is a cruel and destructive force, waiting to obliterate any of my own thoughts on what I imagined was a social life. The week, however, is it's polar opposite—a casual and comfortable friend. And with it homework, guaranteed daily interaction, and a schedule. Welcome, Monday my friend. By my comfort these next days.

Wednesday, February 1, 2006

Wow. Life is such an enjoyable enterprise. Literally everything makes it better, it seems. Of course, I am a naïve fool who has not experienced much in life, but that is my two cents.

August 18, 2005

Today was quite productive. Got up early, ran some errands, did some Internet shopping for cameras and laptops (2 Oxford necessities), read a bit in 1776 (a fascinating read), and helped my mom for a few hours working out playlists and the like for her iPod. The real action began after the dinner meal, when Dad and I headed to Mayfair to hit up the Apple Store. We had this baller of a salesman; Jack was his name, who was important because he impressed the old man. I know this sounds like I stole the next line from Jack but this one is all me baby, these computers basically sell themselves. The things are incredible. Of course the dude helps you in figuring out all the features, but the machine itself is a piece of technological genius. And not too expensive, either. So I'm going to get one. On the way home, there was this beautiful lightning illuminating the knighted cloudy sky, and Dad and I were filled with wonderment. That got me asking him a question, despite already knowing the answer given his profession: what in nature are you most fascinated by? He agreed with the likes of Sophocles:"Numberless are the world's wonders, but none – none more wondrous than the body of man." Me, I love the sky (very general, yes, I know). That canopy never ceases to fascinate me. A starry night always reminds me of my size, or lack thereof. The bright blue of a cloudless summer day could not be recreated by a billion-colored palette. The incredible spectrum that follows the sun as it departs and returns with it every morning is worth getting up in the morning. I told Dawn this summer that if I were ever to think of committing suicide (knock on wood!), the pleasure a sunset/rise gives me is enough to keep me here, amidst all the starvation, war, and famine. Or how about when the clouds gather in such a glorious fashion that one might mistake it for the triumphal re-entry. Sometimes, I am surprised when I don't see cherubim and seraphim blowing trumpets announcing His arrival (they play instruments, right?). But my dad is probably right. Listen to the words of St. Augustine: "A fly is a nobler creature than the sun, because a fly hath life, and the sun hath not." And, what has more life than the new-man, and what is more lifeless than a distant earth covering?

∽

8/20/2005

…... I am going to law school with a "To Be Determined" post-schooling goal. Who does that? I do take comfort in this: several times, I have (for lack of a better term) questioned God directly regarding this thing, sort of asking him if this is what I am supposed to do. And I have been filled with a mysterious peace about it all and left with the answer "Yes" filling my head. Strange, huh? I mean, you know that experiences such as that come few and far-between for a child like me.

∽

8/23/04

I wish I could say so much has happened in the past few days but I cannot. I have watched lots of Olympics, which have been amazing, of course….tonight we had a family dinner. I realized how funny Jeff is. His humor is purely genius. He is witty, quick, and sometimes off-color. His best moments, I feel, are among us—his family. In crowds, usually containing his boyz, he tries too much to raise his volume unnecessarily. Still good, but less classy. Nothing I say at the dinner table compares to his ge-

155

nius. I have learned my role now I think. I will try less to force any humor on the suspecting crowd I call the David L. Larson family.

∞

7/21-22/05

Hi there! It is now Friday. I was tired yesterday and decided that anything I could share could be improved if I delayed my writing about it one more day. You be the judge of whether or not that was a good idea. Real quick, I want to apologize for my handwriting. I mean, look at this trash. It's a pitiful excuse for the written word. I always knew my Dad's was awful (what with him being a physician and all...as though that were a legitimate excuse). Why has that become accepted? "Oh, he's a doctor", we say in explanation. And I'm an astronaut! Who gives a rat's bum? Since when do we afford certain occupations grace in the underperformance of a certain task that improves interaction with all who relate with those belonging to said occupation? I just don't understand why we've come to accept it— this flagrant violation of courtesy for your fellow man. Obviously, I speak as a hypocrite for I, too, belong to membership of that embarrassing and monkey-like club—the illegible penmanshipeers, but at least I don't have a prepared excuse, such as, "Oh, well he's planning on going to law school so it's okay." Or anything else just as arbitrary—"Oh, he used to listen to AC/DC in 7th grade so it's okay." Or, "Oh, well he thinks that green jello, be it apple or lime, doesn't compare with any of the reds—cherry, strawberry, raspberry, even watermelon, which is actually pink, so its okay."

I had hoped my dad's faulted script wasn't hereditary but perhaps that was a mere pipedream. Anyway, this side note turned into a novel, so you have my apologies...

∞

BRAD *went on a single sky-diving adventure along with a couple of his 3rd East Taylor friends. His parents had no knowledge of this until months after his death, but he did document the occasion for us, nonetheless.*

8/27/2005 SKY-DIVING

Anyway, this afternoon we went out to a late breakfast, caught an average movie (The Great Raid), and then hit the road bound for the sky. We arrived at the place at about 3:45, fifteen minutes before our scheduled time. We ended up sitting there for over two hours before commencing (including our second segment of the instructional class that we were not supposed to have to repeat). Anyway, I had Scotty, the Australian dude. He was cool – totally the stereotypical skydiving instructor. He had the tattoos, the crazy attitude, the cool factor, the foul tongue and dirty mind. He was all about it. And I was glad that I did, because Ahern's dude was kind of the one that didn't really fit in. Ouch. Anyway, the trip up in the plane was pretty crazy. We were one thousand feet up and it was already quite high. As in, I couldn't believe we were only one thirteenth of the way up. About five thousand feet, he began to strap me in real tight. And I mean real tight. He gave me the instructions for about the fifth time, which I was fine with. Ahern went first. And I'm glad he did because it was pretty smooth to watch someone jump out of a place like that. He just whipped on out there. Five to seven seconds later, I followed him. Insane. I screamed for the whole minute, which was one of the more stupid things I could have done for two reasons. First of all, it didn't make any difference because no matter how loud I screamed, no one could have heard it. Second of all, my voice is quite sore now. Anyways, he wasn't kidding when he said it would be the fastest minute of my life. The next five or so minutes was the parachuted fall. I made small talk with the dude, but the fun part came when Lentscher's dude maneuvered his chute right next to ours. We exchanged a few "dude, how sweet was that" lines and then parted ways. It was incredibly tight, though. I loved every second of it. Would I do it again? Perhaps, but right now, a hundred and fifty bucks is a lot of cash. Maybe someday.

Sunday, February 26, 2006

Baller day....I sent out a banquet email today, of which I am pretty proud. I really pull out some genius stuff in these emails, I'm telling you. Here it is in its entirety.

From: Larson, Brad
Sent: Sun 2/26/2006 10:55 AM
To: Available Banquet People
Subject: banquet trailblazing

Friends and loved ones:

I am here to make all your banqueting dreams come true. However, as you know, many are called, but few are chosen. And by called, I mean emailed. And by chosen, I mean whoever lets me know the quickest. So holler at me AQAP (as quickly as possible) if you're interested. And by interested, I mean ready and willing to offer up your whole selves as sacrificial banquet workers, giving up your social lives for $5.75 an hour. It's a hard trail, but somebody's gotta blaze it...

Tuesday, Feb. 28th, from 3.15 to 8.15 (I need 2 of you cats)

Monday, March 6th, from 2 to approx. 4.30 (I need 4 or 5 of you jokers)

Saturday, March 11th, starting at 10 am. I need 5 peeps to stay until 2 pm. And 3 more to stay until 3 pm. Make sure you specify whether you'd like to stay for the extra hour or not.

Alright, now it's your turn to get at me...

With passion and vigor,

Bradley J. Larson

March 16, 2006

....I got an encouraging email from Jeff today, telling me that he had been forwarded my latest mass banqueting email from Joe who'd gotten it from Cassidy who'd gotten it from Kendra and that he thought it was the funniest thing he'd ever read. I was a bit embarrassed after that, mostly since I thought that was the worst of those emails I'd sent all year. Here it is:

Banqueting masses,

Don't pretend that I don't know your secrets. Don't think that I am some schmuck, some lowlife, some know-nothing. I know all about your dream to one day be crowned a member of the honorable banqueting royalty. You want to be remembered in the halls of the Arthur L. Hodson Dining Commons, with your names mentioned alongside the greats: the Dave Niffins, the Joe Zimmermans, the Brendan Maloneys of years past. When names like that are mentioned, people bow a knee. (I even saw one dude lay prostrate one time in the wet bar when Joe Z. was brought up.) Those are names that strike a chord in your hearts; I know it and you know it, so there ain't no use denying it. You've been dreaming of banqueting glory since before you were fidgeting around in your mama's tummy. Since before you were even a sparkle in your daddy's eye. And here is yet another opportunity for you to fulfill those lifelong dreams. I should be selling these things for as fast as they're gonna fly off the proverbial shelves.

Thursday, April 6: 4-9 or so. I need 5 of you jokers.
Friday, April 7: 4-10 or sooner. I want 6 of you lucky buggers.
Sunday, April 9: 4-8.30 or 9. Gimme 2 of yours.

I doubt I even have to tell you how hott these tickets are selling. It's comparable to John and George being resurrected and joining with Paul and Ringo for a one night only reunion show at the House of Blues in Chicago. (If that does in fact happen by the way, I guarantee they open with Hard Day's Night.)
Go ahead and hit "Reply" this instant, or else it'll be too late.

In duty to my country,
Bradley J. Larson

EASTER *weekend of 2006 Brad and some of his Taylor friends from 3ʳᵈ East Wengatz traveled to Boston to attend a graduate course vocal recital of Taylor Horner, a good friend and previous 3ʳᵈ East brother. This entry relays a "mishap" that occurred on the way home.*

April 17, 2006

The ride home *(from Boston)* featured one of the trip's highlights. Beeh was quite adamant about the fact that he wanted to "kill the tank" (which was full) before having to stop. It became apparent to me within a few hours that I would not make it. I put it off for a good bit before settling on the fact that I was going to have to urinate into a McDonald's cup (a medium). Remarkably, it was the exact right size. About a half an inch from the top of the cup, I stopped peeing, as my tank was empty. I proceeded to roll down the window, carelessly forgetting an essential element of such a task: putting the top on. In one quick motion, I tossed the cup out the window while the car was going 75 miles per hour. In an instant, everyone and everything in the car were covered by a "warm" shower - pillows, leather seats, and faces included. There was lots of yelling and cursing, and by the end of it, we were in tears. Ironically, we ended up stopping at the next rest stop anyways, just for clean up purposes. It was quite entertaining. Incredibly, I was somehow able to convince Beeh and Jordan that they were 30 and 10 percent at fault, respectively, for their thoughtless decision not to remind me that a top would be necessary. I gladly took the 60% and counted myself fortunate. That was the weekend. We got back at about 8.30 am.

∞

THIS *is an email that Brad, a supervisor and Dining Commons banquet manager, wrote to encourage/coax those workers into volunteering to take advantage of a work opportunity. This also happens to be the request for those workers who were involved in the April 26, 2006 accident.*

From: "Bradley J. Larson"
Date: 22 April 2006 16:32:22
Cc:.edu, Subject: Banquets + U = Happiness

Men and women of Upland:

It has certainly been a long time, hasn't it. (That was a statement of fact, not a question; therefore, no question mark is necessary.) My apologies to all of you whose wallets have been emptied by Spring Break meanderings and Easter vaycay's and the most recent surge in gasoline prices. (We're up to 75 bones a barrel now for Middle East oil. I've been saying it for years: if we simply drilled a bunch of holes in Alaska, we'd be virtually swimming in cheap oil.) Anyways, I know you need currency, and yet again, I am one of the few and proud who are giving you a chance to obtain that legal tender which your heart so deviously desires. I do feel it necessary to remind you, as the author of the book of I Timothy once did: "The love of money is the root of all evil," chapter 6, verse 10.

And now, I present to you BOW, a creative acronym I've developed for this - Banquet Opportunities Week. (Many think this was stolen from the similarly titled World Opportunities Week. Friends, I assure you: this is not so. I came up with this one all by my lonesome.)

Wednesday, April 26: Anyone who wants to go to Ft. Wayne for the afternoon is welcome. You will come in at 1, get paid for any driving time, get a free dinner, and be back by 6 or 7 pm.

Thursday, April 27: Again, a trip to Ft. Wayne. You will leave at 8 am and get back by 4 pm.

Thursday, April 27: Same day but a different job. You can setup for a huge one from 5 to 9 pm.

Friday, April 28: Anyone who can come in for any stretch of time between 10 and 3, let me know. We'd love to have your assistance.

Friday, April 28: A banquet from 4 to 9.45 or so. Should be a calm and intimate affair.

You examine these opp's. You pray about it. You get back to me.

Always and 4ever,   Bradley J. Larson

⌇

THESE *are "Quotable Quotes" that have been assembled from Brad's computer and diaries. Obviously they had a special meaning for him.*

5/2/02 "A mind stretched, never returns to its original shape." Tim Moore (Heritage High School teacher and mentor)

7/6/02 "The only true currency in this bankrupt world is what you share with someone else when you're uncool." Almost Famous

7/8/02 "If you want to improve, be content to be thought foolish and stupid" Some philosopher

7/10/02 "For we are always what our situations hand us; its either sadness Or euphoria." Billy Joel, Summer Highland Falls

8/23/02 "The law brings about wrath, for where there is no law, there is no transgression." Romans 4:15

9/20/02 "Man, you are one twisted _____." "Nope. I'm just an ordinary guy with nothing to lose." Lester Burnam

10/2/02 "If Jesus is God and He died for me, then no sacrifice is too great for me to give to Him." C.T. Studd

12/31/02 "To be born is to be exposed to delights and miseries greater than imagination could have anticipated; that the choice of ways at my cross-road may be more important than we think; and that short cuts may lead to very nasty places." C.S. Lewis

1/12/03 "Either this man was, and is, the Son of God or else a madman or something worse. You can shut Him up for a fool, you can spit at Him, and kill Him as a demon; or you can fall at His feet and call Him Lord and God. But let us not come with any patronizing nonsense about his being a great human teacher. He has not left that open to us. He did not intend to."

"A man who gives in to temptation after 5 minutes simply does not know what it would have been an hour later. That is why, in one sense, bad people know very little about badness.....Christ, because He was the only man who never yielded to temptation, is also the only man who knows to the full what temptation means."

"When we talk of a man doing anything for God or giving anything to God, I will tell you what it is really like. It is like a small child going to his father and saying, 'Daddy, give me a sixpence to buy you a birthday present.' Of course, the father does, and he is pleased with the child's present. It is all very nice and proper, but only an idiot would think that the father is sixpence to the good on the transaction."

   C.S. Lewis, Mere Christianity

"In the absence of any other proof, the thumb alone would convince me of God's existence." Isaac Newton

"The glory of God is a person fully alive."

"Lord, help me begin to begin." George Whitefield.

"Time has no divisions to mark its passage, there is never a thunderstorm or blare of trumpets to announce the beginning a new month or year. Even when a new century begins, it is only we mortals who ring bells and fire off pistols." Thomas Mann

Chapter 9

∞

LETTERS FROM BRAD TO HIS PARENTS

But the seed on good soil stands for those with a noble and good heart, who hear the word, retain it, and by persevering produce a crop.

LUKE 8: 15

THIS *is an entry in Brad's diary:*

1/11/04

Went to church today and Mick spoke about the husband and wife relationship. Listening, I came up with the idea to write letters to my parents about various topics in hopes of them imparting their knowledge and wisdom to me. I hope I go through with it.

It was just a few days later that we received the following letter:

1/13/04

Mom and Dad-

I have a proposal for you. I was daydreaming this past Sunday, and I think this could turn out to be a good idea. I know you guys have a lot of wisdom and knowledge, and that is something I would love for you to share with me. My idea is that I ask you questions about a variety of topics, and you answer them separately, not collectively. I want both of your guy's thoughts and opinions which could differ drastically on certain issues. I think this could best be accomplished through letters, mostly for my benefit. Letters would give me something tangible that I could always keep and treasure. The thing is, this requires much more of an effort on your part. All I have to do is ask the questions but I would appreciate it if you thought out your ideas in detail before putting them to paper. If this sounds like something you could do for your son, he would be thrilled and forever indebted for your efforts. I've thought about this a lot over the past couple days and I think it could be an awesome thing. I'm thinking you would be in on this so I kind of want to get started. So here goes Round One: What do you think of this idea? Be honest. And also, the real question: **What qualities do you think I should look for in a wife?** Remember, since I want both of your thoughts, give individual answers! Don't write these together. I am doing this because I love and respect you. And I know you have a lot to share with me that I probably would never give you a chance to share. Please do this for me. I think I would treasure these letters forever.

Love, Your Son,
Brad

P.S. Dad, be legible.

February 2, 2004

Mom and Dad-

Thank you very much for the letters. I appreciated both the Biblical and practical insights you wrote of. Although I'm not going to elaborate on how much they meant to me here, please know they have had a great impact on me.

And so Round 2 begins. My next question is: **What are your biggest regrets in life?** I know you would like to tell me you have no regrets but that is not true. I even have regrets already, and I am only a sophomore in college. For example, I wish I had been more kind to people in my time at Heritage (*his high school*). I think I probably came off as a jerk a lot of times and I hate myself for it. I wish I had been more generous. Too often my selfish heart has won the battle versus giving. Now, I try to remind myself that money is only money. Do I want to let it control my actions? Maybe your regret is about not being close enough to a sibling or a parent. Or choosing the wrong college. Whatever it is, would you please share it with me? Also share its inverse. The best decision you ever made (or decisions, if several stand out). I await your responses.

Love,
Bradley

⌒⌒

2/29/04

Mom and Dad-

The next topic: finances. **Do you have anything that you would like to share with me regarding financial matters?** I feel I learned a lot through the Bible study I did with the Hawkins this summer. I learned about financial carelessness, being a steward of God, saving, gambling, etc. I already felt that I was fairly responsible with my money but that did open me up to things I hadn't thought of much before. Anyways, I would appreciate your advice. I also have a more specific question within this realm. One that I'm not too excited to ask, but I think it needs to be asked. Do you think you guys pay too much for me? You pay virtually every expense I have—car, car insurance, cell phone, clothes, things here at school, etc. Do you think it is time that at least some of that diminish? As you know, I have plenty of money in that other account from all my summer work. I know guys that manage fine without making as much as I do during the summer. Also, I think it might be time for my allowance to stop. I don't want to sound like I'm ungrateful for your generosity or that I don't like getting $20 once a week. Please don't take it that way. But do you think it might help me make a step toward financial maturity if I depended more on myself, at least in some ways? Car insurance would still be nice, if you deem it fitting, but allowance and cell phone might help me make that step. (I barely use my cell phone; you know that from probably looking at my bills). Please be honest whether you agree or disagree. If this doesn't make sense, I apologize.

Love,
Brad

∞

4/5/04

Mom and Dad-

Round 4 begins. This question is less about imparting wisdom and more about history. **What can you tell me about my family background?** I know virtually nothing of those Larsons and Anklis that came before me. The only thing I really know is that it was the flag of Sweden (I believe) that was on our t-shirts at the Larson family reunion in Door County. Do you guys have family trees or anything like that? I feel embarrassed at the lack of knowledge of such a topic, and I was hoping you could change that. Anything else you think I would find interesting I would love to hear about too. I only know tiny pieces of even your backgrounds, just small stories that you told and I managed to remember. Tell me anything and everything—stories, memories, etc. I would love to hear.

Your son,
Brad

∞

4/25/05

Mom and Pop-

Howdy. Long time no writing. I still don't think I obtained either of your last letters about your heroes. Actually, maybe I did get yours Dad but not Mom's. Here is another letter regardless. **I would like to know**

167

the story of your faith, individually of course. I find it somewhat despicable that I know little to nothing of these stories and for that I apologize. But I am here to rectify such a problem. You may know bits and pieces of my own story, but here it is regardless.

The first time I remember "being saved" was with Bob Conklin at Boy's Club in 4th grade. That was the first night I remember making a decision for Christ. I believe that if I would have died any night after that, I would have been soaring with the angels, as they say. But I don't think I began to "make my faith my own," until say 8th or 9th grade. That was when I first began to develop a personal devotional time every day at the behest of Jeff Nelson (*his high school principal*). I began simply, reading a Proverb a day and picking one verse from it to remember throughout the day. From there, of course, it has grown. And I have as well. Different things have helped to mold me since those humble beginnings. Ones that I can easily point to are teaching Sunday School class for 3 years, my Bible study/relationship with Aalsma, going to college, reading books that challenge my faith and beliefs, my friends at Taylor, my Lighthouse trip, and developing the discipline of fasting. Obviously, everything I've said is incredibly condensed and I would love to expound on such things if you guys are interested. I am just so grateful to have been blessed with 2 parents who love Jesus and set a near flawless example for their three little ones. So thank you from the nethermost of my cardiac chamber (an amusing way to avoid the cliché phrase "from the bottom of my heart").

Love,
Bradley J. Larson

⌒

11/15/05

Mom and Pop-

It has been a long time. But here we are again. Let's jump right in as though we were the local husky boy at the local pool eager to do a cannonball before the teenaged girls go inside because it got cloudy. Question 6:

Excluding family members, who has been the biggest impact upon you as a person? Feel free to give more than one answer.

I could list several people. In high school, Tim Aalsma (*one of his high school teachers*) had an incredible impact upon my person. He made a huge effort to invest time and his life into me and I will always appreciate him for that. He was an incredible instigating force in my developing a real and personal quiet time. Though it may be hard to believe since you haven't seen much progress in this area, he is the reason I have good and meaningful relationships with females. If I have questions about nearly anything or need encouragement, he will not hesitate to give me advice or an uplifting word. And still, no matter how long it has been since I talked to him last, I am always 100% comfortable talking with him. I have few relationships like that. I love Tim Aalsma.

In terms of being someone I want to become (remember, excluding family rule applies ruling out you guys and Jeff), I look at Brent Torrenga (*another of his teachers*). The man is an incredible husband, father, and person. I never cease to be amazed at the manner with which he lives his life. He is humble, selfless, kind, caring, sensitive, and gracious; the list goes on and on. He has been a wonderful example to me. I love Brent Torrenga.

If I want to look at one of my contemporaries, I do not hesitate to say that Mark Van Ryn has changed my life. The reasons are too many to list. He is totally 100% in love with his Savior. He is totally selfless, living out the example of Christ as best I can imagine a lowly human doing. He is respectful of his authorities in a way I've never seen. I have also never ever heard him speak disrespectfully of a girl, which is an incredible feat considering our age and living with 30 other guys. He will not talk about people behind their backs. His love for those in his family has caused me to appreciate my own in so many ways. He is humble. He never uttered a curse word within hearing distance of me. He is incredibly well-liked. I could list many more of the ways he has influenced me but I will hold back. In short, I love Mark Van Ryn.

Please share your thoughts with me

Your son,
Bradley J. Larson

Chapter 10

⁐

FAMILY REFLECTIONS

Dealing with such a catastrophic event has obvious, immediate effects on the lives of each family member. The ripple effects of the loss of Brad will continue for a lifetime. In this chapter, we have included David's and Jeff's eulogies, as well as Sherry's testimony, written two years after the accident. These, and the other writings in this chapter, might give the reader insight into how Brad's family dealt with his loss.

⁐

Dad's Eulogy

Sherry and I want to express our profound gratitude for the outpouring of love, sympathy, and respect that have been demonstrated these past few days for our family. Particular thanks to our special friends and family who have come from all over the country to support us in our profound loss. It is truly humbling and overwhelming. But today is not about us, it is about a very special man, a man who was loved and respected by all who knew him, a man who was not on this earth long enough and yet one who has made an indelible impact on all who knew him that will live well beyond his shortened lifetime.

There are many descriptors that can be applied to Bradley Jesse Larson: servant to all, dependable, disciplined, trustworthy, unassuming, beloved, handsome, respected, frugal, caring, and thoughtful, a "man of his word", smart, witty, a man's man—just plain fun to be round. But he was so much more than that, he was a thinker, someone who truly loved people for who they are. Over the last four days scores of you have come to our home and shared story after story about his selfless acts of kindness, his caring, and his character. As a result, Sherry and I have a new insight into this man we may never have otherwise known. We thank all of you for that. The thing that made Brad so special is that he did not recognize himself as being special. He was a humble young man, three words that don't typically occur in the same sentence in today's culture.

What was it that made Brad tick, what was it that made him so unique? As his Dad, I can't profess to know for sure, but one thing I do know is that he loved the Lord, Jesus Christ, with all his heart, soul, mind, and strength. Based on my personal knowledge and confirmed by what we have heard others say of him, I can honestly say that Brad made every attempt to live his life as Jesus would. He was not perfect, but what was evident to everyone who knew him was his character and integrity, far beyond his twenty-two years.

Although God has taken him back home, he has given all of us the gift of Brad Larson for twenty-two years. When we are given a gift like this, we should use it in a way that would honor Brad. Those of us who knew Brad all received something from him and it is our responsibility to carry that on and pass it to others, just as Brad did with his gifts. We all want to make a difference in the world when we die; we all want to leave a legacy, something by which we will be remembered. But I submit to you that this young man, who died before his time, has left a legacy that those of us three times his age could only aspire to. Brad made a real impact on the lives of all who knew him. Words cannot express how much Brad will be missed, not just by his family but by all of those in the world he touched.

In Brad's death, I, as a father, have a glimpse of the magnitude of God's love for us when he gave us His Son, Jesus Christ, to leave heaven, live on earth, and then see Him die—all for you and me. And because of this act of God, we know that Brad went to heaven the second that truck struck the van. This is a time of mourning, not for Brad, but for us. Our tears reflect what has been torn from us. But let us keep in mind that Brad is now is heaven with his Lord and Savior, Jesus Christ. Sherry and I know that we will join him in heaven on the other side and be with him just as those who have accepted Jesus Christ will be. What a comfort to know that some day we will all be reunited in eternity, for eternity. What I say is true. And it is this truth, and the faith contained therein, that will sustain us in the hard days to come.

Again, thank you for your presence today, your calls, prayers, visits, and many gestures of kindness. Thanks to the many who have filled our home these last few days with stories and reflections of what Brad meant to you and for giving Sherry and I a more complete picture of what a precious person this was. May God receive the glory just as He has received Brad.

April 30, 2006

∞

Jeff's Eulogy

The inadequacy of words was acutely obvious to me on Wednesday night. After speaking with my family, who confirmed that Brad had died, I called a couple of my close friends. Like any good friends would, they expressed remorse and asked me if there was anything they could do. As I hung up the phone, I was struck by a sense of déjà vu. I felt like I had had this conversation before, and after thinking about it, I had. It was when the Packers lost in the playoffs. My friends called me and said things like "Are you okay? I'm there for you. You are in my prayers." At the time, the consolation was appropriate. Now, however, the words felt like someone dropping pebbles down an empty well. You can hear them, but they mean nothing. I felt like new words needed to be invented to describe these feelings of grief.

Over the last two to three years, Brad seemed to be hitting his stride. He excelled in school, he had made great friends, and he was heading to law school after graduation. I was similarly pleased with the development of our relationship as brothers. Whatever differences we had had as teenagers had long been put aside, and we were enjoying some good times. We were both looking forward to the fall, when we would be in Madison, me in a plastic surgery residency and he in law school. A few weeks ago we talked and he made it a point of telling me how much he loved his life right now. He had a lot of friends, a lot of freedom and little responsibility and, as every college student knows, this is the recipe for happiness. Brad was not hitting his stride, though. This was his peak.

This is one reason why my family mourns his death. We know there was more for him in this life. We mourn, too, because we will miss him. We miss his jokes, his laughter and his personality that was loving, gracious and humble. As a brother, I will miss the little things: we loved playing Jeopardy together. We worked out together. We listened to music together.

But while we mourn our loss of him, we do not mourn for his soul. Thanks to his faith in Jesus Christ, we know he is in heaven. And as great as college was for Brad, I'm convinced that heaven is better, although the Jeopardy competition is probably a lot stiffer up there than it is down here.

If I could sum Brad up in a few words, it would be the best man toast that he read at my wedding. It started with him Google-ing "best man toast." He opened with a stupid joke, which was hilarious. He continued with some stories that emasculated me in front of my new wife – also very funny. And, according to the instructions off of "bestmanspeeches.com" he finished with points of sentimentality, closing by telling the crowd that when he grows up, he wants to be just like his big brother. I don't think I have ever heard something so beautiful in my entire life.

To put it simply, Brad was a special kid. There are two more things I would like share with you, the first from myself and the second from Brad. In the last few days, hundreds of people have asked if there is anything they can do. Well, I have finally thought of something. One of my few comforts in this time has been that I know that Brad knew I loved him and so, to anyone in this room who has a brother, tell him today that you love him. And from Brad – if you would have told him on Wednesday morning that this was the day he would die, I know without a doubt that would have been okay with him. He lived his life without regret. And that is why, when I grow up, I want to be like my little brother.

This was our statement at the first anniversary Memorial Service on 4/26/07 at Taylor University.

Ten things we have learned in the past year:

1. To paraphrase C. S. Lewis, "God whispers in your gladness and shouts in your pain". During our time of loss, God has been nearer, bigger, and louder. We have experienced God's unfailing grace and presence through these months. Grace makes good out of a bad situation; good can result from senseless tragedy.

2. ...the value of faith tested and the spiritual growth resulting from it.

3. ...the enormous value and importance of disciplined time in God's Word and prayer in both good times and bad.

4. We have learned how to comfort others as we, ourselves, have been comforted by the Father of compassion and the ministry of His saints.

5. ...the value of intentionality in relationships and within those relationships being transparent, so there can be no reason to have regrets about anything.

6. ...that one of God's most important gifts is relationships with others, starting with Him and the Lord Jesus, for it is through that holy relationship we secure our place in eternity with those who have gone before us.

7. We have chosen to trust in the Lord with all our heart and not lean on our own understanding. Our life was changed forever on April 26, 2006 and our response determines not just the quality, direction, and impact of our lives, but the manner in which others have

viewed us and interacted with us. We have strived to be glorifying to God and honoring to Brad.

8.   ...our lives depend less on circumstances and more on relationships and faith and trust in God..

9.   ...the paradox of gaining through loss, making you more than you thought you might be

10. And finally...how much we want to be like our son today!

Sherry and David Larson

Sherry's Testimony, almost 2 years after the accident

4/25/07

My life was sweet and happy until April 26, 2006. I was raised in a good home, the oldest of 4 children. My Dad owned a small business; my Mother was a stay-at-home Mom. My parents appreciated the importance of their children having a religious foundation so they took my brothers and sister and me to Sunday School, taught us to say our prayers at night, and instilled in us good values.   I accepted the Lord Jesus as my Savior when I was a college student at Michigan State University. I went on to marry David, the man of my dreams (we will celebrate 31 years of marriage next month), and we had 3 smart, attractive children, who became Christ-loving young adults. Ours was a close and happy family. I used to describe my life as "charmed."

But, to borrow the words of the Old Testament figure, Job, "What I feared has come upon me; what I dreaded has happened to me." (Job 3:25) David's and my youngest child, a son, died almost two years ago now. Brad was 22 years old, a senior at Taylor University, a small Christian College, in Upland, Indiana. He was just 3 weeks shy of his college graduation and would have started law school at the University of Wisconsin in Madison in the fall following his graduation.

My husband and I received the call that every parent fears on a Wednesday evening. From the moment we learned there had been an accident involving our son, it was over 4 hours and many phone calls later before we learned from the Chaplain of the Indiana State Police that Brad was among 5 who died at the scene when a semi-truck crossed the median of Interstate-69 in central Indiana and struck a Taylor University van. The driver of the truck fell asleep at the wheel. The van carried 9 students and employees who were returning to Taylor in the early evening after setting up for an honors banquet at a satellite campus. Part of this tragedy made national news. Two blond girls were misidentified at the scene of the accident. One family buried a young woman not their daughter, and another family nursed a comatose young woman thinking she was their daughter, but who was not. The mistake was not discovered until 5 weeks after the accident.

As long as I live, I will never forget my husband saying, "Brad is dead." There are no words to describe the shock, the anguish, the disbelief, the sorrow, the confusion, the heartache of the next hours and days and weeks. How could THIS happen to my wonderful family? Even today, I often ask myself that same question. But, on the first morning after learning that our son had gone to heaven, I felt I had a choice to make, and I wrote in my journal, "I will trust in the Lord with all my heart and will not lean on my own understanding..." a proverb I had memorized many years ago. I felt that God was asking me to live, by faith, all that I have professed to be true over the years. I have come to believe that faith and trust are what God honors most, especially in the face of tragedy that we cannot possibly understand this side of heaven. Again, to use the words of my Old Testament Friend, Job, "Though He slay me, yet will I trust in him."

Let me tell you a little bit about Brad. We have received scores of letters from his friends, their parents, former teachers and others telling us of the impact Brad made on their lives. Please allow me to share some of these remarks with you as they describe Brad much more objectively than I can. I have chosen excerpts from one letter that is representative of all the others.

"Brad smiled and laughed and hugged me every time he saw me. He is the person in my life that was always most excited to see me. And the funny thing is, I know I wasn't the only one he did that to."

"He was so disciplined."

"He was a model that I wanted to strive after in living above reproach."

"He was amazing with words. His emails were all instant classics."

"He did everything to the fullest: Everything: arguments, NBA stats, games, conversations about anything."

"He lived with a sense of urgency. A couple of his last words in response to one friend wanting to watch a movie, he said, 'No man, we gotta make the most of our days.' And after a Numa video in which a tragic death happened at the end, Brad said, 'Wow, you just never know. You just never know how much time you have.'"

"He would ask more guys how they were doing than anyone I know."

"One of the guys saw him praying for over an hour on his knees just several days ago."

"Bible reading every night my freshman year."

"He loved me and he was genuine."

"He was smart…school work was never an issue. He just got it done. So many people have told me how Brad touched their life and all I can do is nod my head because I know exactly what they are talking about. Brad would make you feel like the center of the universe each time he talked to you. He would turn you toward himself and just listen and offer amazing advice."

"Brad was a servant. For me, he was always the first one to come and ask me what he could do to help. 'Tell me what you need and I'll do it.' So few people are like that."

These remarks are just a small picture of what Brad was like.

Through all this, God has been gracious to me. He has blessed me with what I have termed "tender mercies," gifts from Him that prove to me He loves me in the midst of this tragedy. "Hear me O Lord, for your loving-kindness is good; turn to me according to the multitude of your tender mercies." (Psalm 69:16) Tender mercies have come to me in many forms not the least of which are dear caring friends who have loved and served me and my family through this trial. When I wondered how my broken heart could continue to beat, my friends were near, my precious MOPS were near, each of them a tender mercy. We learned from the driver of the Taylor van who survived the accident that Brad and the others in the back of the van were talking and laughing as the van was struck by the truck.

We believe they went to heaven laughing and talking, a tender mercy! In the first days after Brad died, I prayed for a Baltimore Oriole to come to my new bird feeder as a sign from God that He loved me and was caring for me. I didn't think I was asking too much—it was May, not January! But instead, God sent a peacock! "To Him who is able to do immeasurably more than all we ask or imagine…" (Eph. 3:20), another tender mercy. Remarkably, this happened again last spring. I put out my Baltimore Oriole feeder and my oranges and prayed for a Baltimore Oriole. I never saw even one. But I did see a peacock, a fancy male peacock strutting his stuff along a road in the middle of nowhere in northern Wisconsin over the Memorial Day weekend!

Four months after the accident I found 9 handwritten journals, that unbeknown to us, Brad had been keeping since high school. We found the last year of his life journaled on his computer. He left an additional prayer journal, intimate conversations he shared with His Lord. These are the most tender of mercies! We believe Brad was divinely inspired to journal so faithfully that we might have the legacy of his thoughts and prayers. We have His testimony all written out; it ends with Jeremiah 29:11. "For I know the plans I have for you," declares the Lord, "plans to prosper you and not to harm you, plans to give you a hope and a future." A tender mercy. I have a list of his friends whom Brad wanted to stand up in his wedding and why. Brad had few dating relationships, but I have a letter he wrote to his future wife to be read on their wedding night. I have a series of letters my husband and I exchanged with Brad in recent years. He asked us thought-provoking questions and we replied. Brad said he wanted to tap into our wisdom. Brad in turn answered those same questions for us. I consider those precious letters tender mercies. I have, in Brad's own words, from an email exchange with a friend, how he wanted to be remembered at his funeral. "I want my parents to think I was a good son, my siblings to know I love them and my friends to miss me." A tender mercy. I have a post-it note on my bathroom mirror in Brad's hand that says. "I love you." It is signed Brad. I have a new dear friend, another Mom who also "lost" a precious son, Clint, 3 months before Brad died. You may know Mona Erickson. Mona is fond of saying, "We did not 'lose' our boys! We know exactly where they are!" Mona's friendship is a tender mercy.

Part of Brad's story is also a love story. A recurrent theme in his journal are prayers for his future wife. A recurrent name in his diaries since his freshman year is Laura Van Ryn. It was no secret that Brad loved Laura. It was uncertain what Laura's feelings were for Brad, except that they shared a close friendship throughout their 4 years at Taylor. Brad and Laura went to heaven together on April 26th, 2006. This is a tender mercy.

After Brad died, we found a pen tucked in his Bible marking Psalm 139 with verse 16 (among others) underlined. "All the days ordained for me were written in your book before one of them came to be." We believe that it was Brad's time to go to heaven, and we believe even Brad had an understanding of the frailty of life. But as we learned how he impacted so many people so positively, I kept thinking how much more he could have impacted people for God's kingdom, especially at the University of Wisconsin, but on into his future too. He was gifted and good, a role model for his peers, influential for Christ. The "why now" question was so troubling for me until one day it dawned on me that the Lord Jesus died young too. He was only 33—how much more could He have impacted the world if He had lived longer! Then I ran across the following in two books I read, The Vanishing Power of Death and One Minute After You Die, both by Erwin Lutzer, a Moody Bible Institute teacher and author.

From the former book: *"Jesus died according to the purposes of divine providence, not the whims of the envious religious leaders or cowardly Romans. Just so, you and I will die; not according to the will of an erratic drunk cruising along the highway; not according to the will of a painful disease. Any one of these might be the chariot God will use to take us to Himself, but be assured we will die under the good hand of God's providential care. We will pass through the curtain according to God's clock, not the timetable of random fate."*

Lutzer elaborates on this further in One Minute After You Die. Here are just a few sentences: *"Christ died young, but His work was finished. We don't have to live a long life to do all that God has planned for us to do. Some of God's best servants have died at an early age... They too have finished the work God gave them to do.*

... let us boldly say that even when a believer is murdered by evil men... such a one dies according to the providential plan of God. If Christ, who was brutally murdered by jealous religious leaders, died as planned by God, why should we think that a believer who is gunned down in a robbery is any less under the care of the Almighty? Car accidents, heart attacks, cancer--all of these are the means used to open the door of heaven to the children of God. The immediate cause of our death is neither haphazard nor arbitrary. The One who knows the number of hairs on our head and sees the sparrow fall has the destiny of every one of our days in His loving hands."

It hit me like a ton of bricks that Brad had accomplished all that <u>God</u> had planned for him, not what <u>I</u> thought he might accomplish had he lived longer. <u>This</u> has given me peace and comfort, especially when I remind myself that His plans are not my plans; His ways are not my ways. "...now, we see in a mirror dimly, but then face to face. Now I know in part; then I shall know fully..." (I Cor.13:12)

Through my grief journey this past two years, I have depended on these truths... The Lord himself goes before me. He will never leave me nor forsake me. (Deut. 31:8) God is near to the broken-hearted. "The Lord has heard my cry for mercy...." (Ps. 6:9)

I know this to be true...God's grace is sufficient for each day. (II Cor. 12:9) I grieve, but not as those who have no hope. (I Thess. 4:13)

I know this to be true...there is nothing more important than securing our place in eternity. "..if you confess with your mouth, 'Jesus is Lord,' and believe in your heart that God raised him from the dead, you will be saved." (Romans 10:9) Brad understood this, and he embraced His Savior.

I know this to be true..."I know that My Redeemer lives." (Job 19:25) I share that belief with my suffering Friend, Job. I know that life on this earth is but a vapor when we look at eternity. And, I know that in the end Jesus Christ is victorious!

My walk through this tragedy has not been one of total surrender. I have wrestled with God, I have anguished over questions that have no earthly answers. I can still cry myself to sleep when I think of my broken family. I become discouraged, and then I remind myself of God's promises and His tender mercies to me. But, I have the promise of the Lord Jesus

Himself that Brad is well and safe in His arms: On the day the Lord Jesus was crucified, he said to his neighbor on the cross, "I tell you the truth, today you will be with me in paradise." (Luke 23:43). And I will see my precious son again.

January 2007

Updated March 2008

∞

Sixteen months after the accident, the driver of the truck, charged with five counts of second degree manslaughter, pleaded guilty and the families of the deceased were given an opportunity to make a statement at the sentencing of the driver. This was the statement Sherry read in the courtroom.

Because of the deliberate actions of a truck driver who chose to disobey the law, April 26, 2006 is a date that will be written on the hearts and minds of many people for years to come. It is a date that is written on five grave stones. It is a date that will be memorialized with a prayer chapel at Taylor University. It is the date when five innocent children of God were taken to their Maker. One of these precious ones was our youngest son, Brad.

There are no words to describe the shock, the bewilderment, the anguish, the disbelief, the heartache of the past months since our son went to heaven. He was just three weeks shy of his college graduation and would have started law school this past fall at the University of Wisconsin. Because of the willful carelessness of this truck driver, we have been robbed of seeing Brad become a professional, a husband and father, a productive citizen. We are forever deprived of the company that mothers and fathers, sisters and brothers, friends, enjoy with their loved ones. Our close and happy family has been forever broken. Brad will never be more than a memory here on earth to those of us who loved him.

David and I were so proud to be Brad's parents. He was sweet and thoughtful. He was smart and athletic. He was well-liked by everyone he came in contact with. He loved life; he loved his brother and sister, his friends; he loved the Lord. An entry in his journal written two months before he was killed reads, "I am loving life right now...I go to bed each night wondering if it would be possible for my life to be more enjoyable..." He was gifted and good, a role model for his peers. He was admired by the students and faculty he met during the fall semester at Oxford University in England, in addition to those he came in contact with at Taylor University. He was loved and respected by those he met during the summers he spent as a counselor at the Upper Peninsula Bible Camp. He is remembered by those he served in India while on a mission trip in January of 2005. We have scores of letters from his friends, their parents, teachers and others telling us of the impact Brad made on their lives and sharing their heartbreak over his untimely death. Brad is safe and well in heaven with our Lord. All of us left behind are the real victims of the actions of this truck driver.

Ultimately, one day, each of us will stand before God to answer for our actions in this life. But today, we are here to ask that earthly justice be assigned for the careless and negligent actions of the man who was responsible for the deaths of our son and the others. Every day we are faced with choices. Most of the choices we make are of little importance. But the choice the truck driver made on the evening of April 26, 2006, to drive his truck beyond the limits of the law, was a selfish and reckless choice that took five innocent lives and left behind five broken families. He should be penalized to the fullest extent of the law.

Sherry A. Larson   David L. Larson, M.D

Chapter 11

∽

GLOSSARY

RECOGNIZING *that there are people of different ages and generations who will read this little book, we have provided a glossary to help guide you through your reading.*

A

Apt   Apartment where Taylor classmates (Laura Van Ryn, Sara Schupra, Christine Cleary) lived a few blocks off campus

Aaron Bear   A childhood friend, Aaron Hawkins, a Heritage High school classmate

Aalsma   Tim Aalsma, Heritage School teacher, mentor, and close friend, also Aalz, 'Sma

Ahern   Mark Ahern, a 3rd East Brother

Aiden   Brad's 8 year old cousin

Air band   A group of people playing imaginary musical instruments, as in "air guitar". A contest can become very sophisticated with choreography and elaborate costumes

B

BT   Brent Torrenga, a Heritage high school teacher who Brad admired

baller   an adjective used to describe something that is very enjoyable; synonym: awesome

banquets   the last two years at Taylor, Brad worked at Dining Commons banquets to make a little money for himself, rather than accept money from his parents

Beeh   Bryan Beeh, a classmate at Taylor

Bellitos	Matt and Becky Bellito, best friends of Jeff and Becky and Taylor University alums
Berg	Ryan Bergman, a 3rd East Brother
Bo	Brittany Head, a Taylor and UPBC friend
Bogs	Nate Bogdanovich, a classmate at Heritage Christian High
Botso	Zan Bozzo, a 3rd East Brother
Boyers	Luke Boyers, a 3rd East Brother and Brad's roommate for his sophomore and junior years
Britto	Brittany Long, a fellow Taylor student
Brucer	Tim Bruce, a close Heritage High School friend
bubbly	soda that was used in celebration activities on 3rd East

C

Celby	Celby Hadley, a 3rd East Brother
Club 336	a room on 3rd East Wengatz which was the site of certain wing activities
Club 31:1	a group of Heritage Christian High boys, headed by Brad, who tried to follow in the steps of the biblical figure Job, who in Job 31:1 said, "I made a covenant with my eyes not to look lustfully at a girl."
convo	conversation
Corduan	Winfried Corduan, PhD, one of Brad's favorite philosophy professors at Taylor

D

Dana	Dana Pietrangelo, a Heritage high school friend
Dawnie	sister, Dawn
devo'ed	past tense of devo (a coined verb meaning to have a devotion with a friend)
devos	devotions
Dewey	The house where Laura VanRyn, Christine Cleary and Sara Schupra lived
Dubski	sister, Dawn
DV	Don Van Ryn, Laura's father

E
el Capitan   Jon Chacko, a 3rd East Brother

F
Flink   Mike Flink, another 3rd East brother

G
Gladley   a nickname for Jason Ladley, 3rd East Brother

H
Hoe's   Ivanhoe's Ice Cream Shop, a favorite of Taylor University students, located in Upland, Indiana
hotness   an adjective applied to something very attractive (e.g. female)
hoss   descriptor of something (or something) of great significance

I

J
Jake   Jake Andersen, Heritage High School friend
Jake   Jake Findley, a 3rd East Brother
Jamie M.   Jamie Miller, Heritage High School friend
Jamie H.   Jamie Hishmeh, a Heritage High School friend
Jess   Jessica Dennis, a Taylor classmate
Jules   Julie Barrett, a Taylor and UPBC friend

K
Kenny   Kenny Van Ryn, Laura's brother
Kludt   David Kludt, a Heritage classmate and "We the People" competitor
Kumer   Matt Kumershek, a Heritage High School classmate

L
Laur   Laura Van Ryn
Liski   Lisa Van Ryn, older sister of Laura

Lor   Laura VanRyn

M

Malvig   Jon Malvig, teacher and friend from Heritage High School
Marky   Mark Van Ryn, brother of Laura and 3rd East Brother (also, Squizz, Squirrel)
Melv   Tim Melville, a childhood friend and Heritage Christian classmate
Meredith   Heritage High School classmate and fellow "We the People" competitor
money ($)   descriptor of a positive event or fortunate coalescence of occurrences
Moose   Scott Barrett, a 3rd East Brother

N

Nelson   Jeff Nelson, the principal at Heritage High School
Nooma   a DVD series, produced by Rob Bell, commonly used in Christian circles to demonstrate basic concepts of Christian belief

O

OC   out of control
opps   opportunities (e.g. there are great opps in a proposal)

P

P-Diddy   Preston Cosgrove, a 3rd East Brother
pape   paper, as in a paper written for a class
Peebs   John Peebles, a 3rd East Brother
peeps   people
pumping   lifting weights , as in "pumping iron"

Q

R

Raul (also Raoul)   Marc Belcastro, 3rd East Wengatz friend

S

SBTB   "Saved by the Bell", a television show

Shoops   Sara Schupra Van Winkle, a Taylor classmate and roommate of Laura Van Ryn

Spiegese   Jim Spiegel, PhD, one of Brad favorite teachers and the man who mentored him as a result of the 12/3 incident

Steedj   Stephen Downy, a 3rd East Wengatz Brother

Sooz (Suz)   Suzie Van Ryn, mother of Laura Van Ryn and co-director, with her husband, Don, of the Upper Peninsula Bible Camp (UPBC) where Brad was a counselor for two summers during college

sick game   term of admiration for excellence at a given task, as in "He has sick game in basketball."

T

T-cell   Taylor Horner, a 3rd East Brother

tight   a descriptor of something that is a very neat or exciting occurrence

Torrenga   Brent Torrenga, one of Brad's favorite teachers at Heritage High School

Trinkl   Jon Trinkl, a high school friend

U

UPBC   Upper Peninsula Bible Camp, a camp where Brad was a counselor for the two summers after his sophomore and junior years of college

V

Vance   Alan Vance, Brad's basketball coach at Heritage high school

W

WWJD — What Would Jesus Do?

Westie — Weston Krider, a 3rd East Brother

X

Y

Yet-face — Andy Yetman, a 3rd East Brother

yogs — yogurt

Yord — Jordan Hawkins, Brad's oldest friend and 3rd East Brother

Z

Zan — Alexander Bozzo, a 3rd East Brother

Zimmy Jimmerman — Jimmy Zimmerman, a 3rd East Brother